10-MINUTE TREATS

SEVENTEEN SHORT STORIES

Bernard Shevlin

Oakamoor
Publishing

Published in 2017 by Oakamoor Publishing, an imprint of Bennion Kearny Limited.

Copyright © Oakamoor Publishing

ISBN: 978-1-910773-51-2

Published by Oakamoor Publishing, an imprint of Bennion Kearny Limited
6 Woodside
Churnet View Road
Oakamoor
ST10 3AE
United Kingdom

Dedicated to "Jackie"; a wonderful stranger whose steadfast support made this book possible; everyone needs a "Jackie" in their life and I feel singularly blessed.

Table of Contents

An idealistic community flees violence and global warming by constructing a huge, mobile artificial island and establishing idealised standards of philosophy and behaviour from its citizens; will the citizens of the New World find this enough? (Reading Time: 10 minutes 2 seconds)

A very boring man has an episode of amnesia, diagnosed as TGA (Transient Global Amnesia), and becomes alarmed as he slowly discovers what happened during his memory blank. (Reading Time: 5 minutes 7 seconds)

A power-mad landowner is forced to face the prospect of his death and the equally terrifying idea that his properties will be owned by someone else. (Reading Time: 12 minutes 22 seconds)

An innocent ice skater is invited to the prom by the most eligible boy in the county; he seems just too good to be true and she falls in love with him, but his agenda might be rather underhand. (Reading Time: 19 minutes 7 seconds)

As people become increasingly inept and apathetic about communication with each other, Vega takes a solitary journey to the home of advanced robotics as she tries to get away from all human contact. (Reading Time: 8 minutes 15 seconds)

An alcoholic doctor encounters a strange man while trying to cope with a beautiful young woman who steals his heart. (Reading Time: 14 minutes 48 seconds)

A poor slum-dwelling boy discovers the beauty of the wilderness and is overwhelmed by seeing a wild cougar, an experience which shapes his future. (Reading Time: 8 minutes 20 seconds)

"Inseparable" twin boys finally have to go their separate ways when the handsome and gifted one is adopted by an adoring family, leaving the other desolate in the orphanage and trying to put his life together. (Reading Time: 11 minutes 6 seconds)

A young woman is trapped alone in a dying valley and the only escape is through a tunnel full of terrors and unknown perils. She is prepared as best she can be, but is it possible to survive the tunnel? (Reading Time: 11 minutes 37 seconds)

At the farthest reaches of space exploration, a strange phenomenon occurs in which travellers go insane. Dare we risk our brightest and best to unlock its dark secrets? (Reading Time: 5 minutes 52 seconds)

When a Master Criminal chooses to retire, he decides that the only fitting end to his career would be to attempt an incredibly difficult burglary. (Reading Time: 9 minutes 56 seconds)

* * *

These estimates of 'time-to-read' are based on the average reading time of 300 words per minute; but if, dear reader, you take a little longer, I would be very grateful!

Thanks to so many friends and relatives who I bullied into reading and criticising the earlier drafts. Especially: Pauline, Sigurd, Ian, Jane, Carol, Martin, Paul, Bianca, Steph, Saul and Henry

And above all to

James – my publisher – whose wisdom and patience have been beyond anything one could reasonably expect!

For other stories by Bernard Shevlin, plus reader queries, comments, author discussions, and more, visit:

www.BennionKearny.com/BernardShevlin

The Teapot

Sadly this is a totally true story.

It was my early days in rural general practice, trying to do a job I found virtually impossible. I would see over 60 patients per day in my "surgeries" (clinics), we would do sessions at a local prison and at a local hospital for the mentally handicapped, we were on call every second or third night with weekend surgeries, home deliveries, "minor" surgery, terminal care responsibilities and "call-outs" to all kinds of "emergencies". Couple these with the fact that I had no training for general practice – nil – so the feeling of being totally overwhelmed was perhaps understandable.

Yet the very worst – and most resented part of my work – were the "house calls"; nowadays they call them "home visits" which sounds a lot more patient- friendly, but I spat out the words "house calls" with some venom, as they were nothing at all to do with "real medicine". In fact a lot of these requests were a hangover from the pre-NHS days when important folks who could afford to do so would "send for the doctor"; naturally patients believed that they would be entitled to this service at the inception of the NHS, whether or not they could have made the trip to the doctor or not. As such the "excuses" for such requests included "no transport" and "not feeling well enough" as if feeling poorly would prevent their travelling to the hospital! The very worst part of all, though, was that I didn't feel like a proper doctor when I did "house-calls" as I was rarely able to do the examinations and tests that would help to find treatable pathology and arrange for it to be sorted.

***

Then, one day, I was asked to see an 84-year-old lady – yet again - who, as was her custom, was in bed when I arrived, like a royal personage in her estate.

As always I suppressed my resentment with a false smile, refused her offer of a cup of tea and was about to beat as

1

hasty a retreat as possible when I noticed it: a barely discernible ulcer with a rolled-up edge on her forehead – a classical BCC – a basal cell carcinoma (rodent ulcer) which could be cured easily. For once I felt like I was a "proper" doctor, making an astute early diagnosis and saving a life. I told her that I would refer her to the hospital and that this needed to be dealt with or it would keep on growing until it ate into her skull and brain (my bedside manner was still in its infancy). For once I left her domain feeling I had done something useful.

**

I didn't see her for a couple of months; presumably, the house call requests had been fielded by my partner. When she did "summon me" once more, I was horrified that the lesion was still sitting there on her forehead.

"Did they not remove it at the hospital?" I asked with some concern.

"I didn't go to the hospital," she finally admitted.

"Did you receive the appointment?" I asked, concerned that my referral letter had somehow gone astray.

"Yes, but I don't want to go to hospital," she said.

I was dumbstruck: this crazy old woman had refused my advice, and my offer of a cure had been spurned.

As usual, I suppressed my annoyance with a wry smile, while muttering something about 'It's your choice' and making an exasperated exit.

**

Over the following years, I saw her many times; on each occasion offering to refer her for surgery should she want it. Each time she demurred, and each time I noticed the skin cancer grow a little bigger. Eventually, she had a special "hat" made to cover the huge ulcer which had obeyed my prophecy and was slowly eating into her skull and beyond. By now I was reconciled to her 'rejection' and indeed had probably become a little more civil to this very 'single-minded' old lady.

***

Then, one evening as I was about to go home after a particularly challenging evening surgery, she phoned in asking for a "home visit." As usual, there seemed no particular valid reason for the call, and I sped off with even more resentment than usual.

The visit went as always, leaving me unable to discern why she had made such a late request for a visit. I was about to leave when she pointed to a rather beautiful china teapot:

"Doctor, I would like you to have this," she said smiling.

I was desperate to get home and bring the conversation to a speedy end:

"Another time," I said with my usual false smile.

***

When I arrived at surgery the next morning, I was horrified to learn that the old lady had died during the night. Like all young doctors, I felt an immediate anxiety at the unexpectedness of the death, but of course, there would be no repercussions as I could easily complete a death certificate and there would be no problems with the relatives or indeed the coroner as my medical behaviour was beyond reproach.

It was only later, as I reflected on the case and shared it with my wife that she rather astutely pointed out:

"She just wanted to say goodbye and thank you… you really should have accepted the teapot."

***

Over the following months and years, I thought many times about the old lady and her teapot, and began to recognise the wisdom of my wife's comments and indeed began to feel a little guilty. In spite of my 'brusqueness,' I had been an important person in this lady's life, and I had denied her last

3

request – her last gesture of friendship to me – the gift of the teapot.

I slowly improved with time in general practice by learning from my 'mistakes' – yes, of course, on clinical matters, but even more about breaches of 'kindness.' And it is these latter breaches which hurt the most as I become older; if only I could go back and do things differently...

I never did receive the teapot, by the way: I certainly didn't deserve it, but the old lady gave me a lot more than a teapot - a painful lesson that will live with me for the rest of my career in medicine.

Bernard Shevlin

Breakfast

Doctor Michael Bullivant, smilingly referred to as "The Crazy Doctor" by his patients and close friends, sat down to breakfast; to stay in such a sumptuous hotel was a rare treat and one of the real perks of speaking at a Medical Convention. He was the first to arrive, as usual, as it was always fun to watch as people came in and observe the many secrets they accidentally gave away about themselves.

"Good morning sir; you are the early bird today," the waitress smiled. He noted the forced professional friendliness to the total stranger and the immaculately positioned uniform (she really valued and needed this job), the old, scuffed shoes (spent all her money on her kids), the almost completely faded bruise around the left eye (abusive, right-handed husband) and the slight nervous tic which betrayed the stresses in her life. He would have her attention for just one sentence – just one sentence to make her feel better about herself:

"Your children so love and appreciate you," he said with emotion, holding her gaze and speaking with total conviction.

"Really?" she asked with some bewilderment.

"Yes, they really do!" he added with a professional certainty she could not challenge. She would be significantly happier for the rest of the morning without knowing quite why… but that was how things were:

'If a patient does not feel better after seeing a doctor, then that doctor is no true physician.'

If you substitute 'person' for 'patient' you have a philosophy of life – that Happiness is infectious, like a wonderful benign virus and we should all be part of the epidemic.

'Surround yourself with Happy People and make people who surround you happy.'

***

A slim, athletic–looking woman entered, wearing expensive one-way sunglasses, 'designer' jeans and (paradoxically) old and foreign-looking sandals; her gait was rather macho and confident, and she put Michael in mind of an off-duty Italian waiter. She sat on the opposite side of the room with a similar view - the other perfect vantage point - and glanced at him with some displeasure, maybe regretting that she had not arrived earlier to be the first customer.

The next entrant was a rather overweight middle-aged man; he looked flushed. He had male-pattern baldness, expensive jewellery and had the facial expression of an insecure alpha male. The designer shirt was short-sleeved to show his developed, muscular arms and the right side of his shirt clung slightly more to his chest than the left. 'Poor guy' thought Michael, 'No-one ever wins in a battle with age. The flush will be from a combination of his CCB (for his blood pressure) and the Viagra he took earlier so he could satisfy his latest girlfriend. He also uses topical testosterone gel which has stuck his shirt to the right side of his chest.'

Michael looked forward to the arrival of the woman who would attest (or maybe not) to the accuracy of his 'reading.'

Next came a middle-aged couple; she had a striking appearance with expensively done hair, false eyelashes, a stunning opulent figure and a short skirt – perhaps a little too short for her age. As they sat down, she reached down and scratched at the tattoo of a boxer on her lower leg.

'Ah,' thought Michael, 'itchy tattoo, therefore slight infection, therefore recent… why would a middle-aged lady have a tattoo of a boxer on her leg? Recent infidelity of husband? The tattoo makes a statement of anger and independence, and she dresses up to keep off the rivals?' She also accompanies him wherever she can, with all the non-verbal cues of "My property – keep off!" Michael smiled; some marriages end up as prisons. As he looked up he saw the woman in jeans smiling too; what did that mean?

Shortly, the bejewelled man's partner came in; at first glance, she looked stunning with the perfect sun tan, expensive blow-dry, designer dress and tell-tale red sole of Louboutin – everything radiating expense and indulgence. She put her arm around him and gave him a kiss. He reciprocated by putting his hand proprietarily on her rear; the deal was clear - that he paid heavily for her validation of his manhood. The expensive new bracelet and matching earrings had probably clinched the deal.

Michael almost laughed out loud, and when he looked across the room, the woman in jeans was also laughing. He began to have a theory.

***

"May I join you?" Michael asked with a smile.

She stared at him for a long 10 seconds.

"Why not?" she said with a superior, amused smile.

"Can I take that as a compliment?" he enjoined.

"Not really," she replied, "but maybe you will entertain me for a short time and satisfy some curiosities."

"Curiosities about what? About me personally?"

"Hardly! You are a fairly open book. You are about 40-years-of-age, sufficiently unconventional that you have your BMJ with you to compensate for your eccentric behaviour and give you 'respectability.' You are heterosexual, but not a big womaniser (dull clothes, crumpled shirt, wearing bedroom slippers for god's sake), probably married, my guess would be to a disabled wife (no fit wife would let you out dressed like that) to whom you have some loyalties. You are probably up-to-date on Medicine, a pisco-vegetarian (I noticed your choice of food), too tender-hearted to kill animals, love children, though probably none of your own. Patients probably adore you and administrators and politicians detest you and don't invite you to serve on committees or give you titles. You are probably at this convention to give a lecture, and your topic will probably be highly controversial. You are attracted to me because you can probably tell that I too am an APW (Advanced People Watcher)."

"So what is your curiosity about me?"

She stared at him with some interest but scarcely concealed condescension:
"What have you got on me?" she finally asked, only partially concealing her low expectations of the answer.

"Okay," began Michael. "You are about 29-years-old, in a relationship with a very feminine woman, who clearly did a wonderful job of ironing your shirt. You are a little restless and would like a fling with someone else. You are very fit, do weight training and long-distance running. However, from the way you walked in, you have a left calf strain, probably about a week old. You looked it up on the web and made your own felt pad to put under your heel to raise it – as advised by the experts. This tells me you seek control, dominance, and power over situations; you don't even like to seek a medical opinion. You dislike men, probably because of a previous abusive relationship. You have fantastic potential but will never realise all of it because of the sad emotional traumas from your past which you are unwilling or unable to exorcise."

She smiled and seemed to relax.

"You are good," she said, offering her hand.

"I'm Antonia, Toni for short."

"Dr. Michael Bullivant, Dr. for short."

"What do you make of that man over there?" She nodded her head in the direction of a newcomer.

Michael looked at him for a few moments.

"He has just had a shower and has been training – probably running – this morning. The paradox is that he smokes which you can tell from his complexion and the faint nicotine stains on his fingers. So who has enough willpower to exercise so assiduously yet can't stop smoking? He is an addictive personality, and last time he tried to stop smoking he probably put on a lot of weight. This makes him vulnerable and a man needing stability. I am surprised that he does not have a partner… maybe she'll come down later. I expect someone rather unremarkable… a woman with whom he will feel totally safe; she will adore him and give him stability in his life."

Toni smiled, stood up and went over to the man. They exchanged a few words and she returned.

"Bingo," she said: "6k this morning; I asked him where he had run as I too was a runner. He has cut down to 12 cigarettes per day. You are good."

Then in came a beautiful, mixed-race woman, who kissed the man lovingly on the cheek and sat down next to him, sitting a rather fidgety 7-year-old boy opposite her.

Michael put his head in his hands in mock shame:

"You weren't wrong, really," Toni enjoined. "His wife (big wedding ring visible) clearly needs him to help bring up this troublesome child from a previous relationship; she needs someone who she can count on and who needs her. It all looks different but is really the same."

"Yes, he looks like an ADHD kid, and he would be the perfect father; in fact, they are a perfect couple!"

"Indeed, quite romantic really. Anything else on me?"

Michael thought for a few moments.

"You have recently lost weight (obvious from the alteration in your belt – the most frayed eye is two notches up) so about 20 lbs! Quite a lot! You have an underactive thyroid and overdose yourself with thyroxine (slight tremor but you aren't anxious and you're drinking chamomile tea so it's not caffeine-related). Doctors generally under-dose with thyroxine, so this has been done at your instigation. This has helped you lose weight, which you are rather thrilled about as your polycystic ovary syndrome feels a lot better and you have (nearly) stopped shaving. You feel better than you have felt in a long time and you have come on this course to have a romantic liaison with a new 'filly.' You are also a rather militant feminist and fairly political and have come especially to hear the Kovalov lecture later this morning."

She laughed and clapped her hands in mock but generous applause.

Then after a slight pause.

"Aren't you curious about the Kovalov lecture?" she asked.

"I can guess the content: recent defector from Eastern Europe, taking the lid off human rights abuses, amoral medical personnel in the pay of the state, etc... but I will be coming."

He paused.

"Will you be coming to my lecture this afternoon?" he added.

She looked at him quizzically.

"Maybe... If I don't find my filly!" she smiled teasingly.

"And I'll buy you dinner if I am at a loose end," added Michael with a smile, which froze on his face as a newcomer walked in, looked around, carefully chose a seat, sat down, and imperiously ordered the waiter over.

The waiter looked scared as he wrote down the man's order; half way through the order, the waiter was pushed to one side as another man appeared, wearing a red necktie. He showed three fingers to the seated man and sat across the room. There were nods of acknowledgement, but no smiles.

"Okay," said Toni, "Do your stuff."

"Right," began the doctor, "the most striking thing about him is his bright red hair which is not his natural colour, is recently and rather badly done – certainly not in a Western Salon – and seems to be in contrast to the rest of his persona. But why? My guess is that it is for identification purposes. The sun-weathered skin could well fit with time spent at sea, and the earrings would also fit with that. The scar on his neck is called a keloid scar and is probably from a knife injury, but his entire manner and face are those of a man who deals in confrontation. The man in the red necktie is an associate, probably his boss and the sign was an instruction, yet they don't want to be seen together… Odd! Also, just look at that lycra top! How out of character! My guess is that he is wearing it to hide tattoos on his arms which might totally give him away. The way he walked in, the way he checked the exits and chose his table, the way he looked around the room with a vigilant snarl and the way he ordered the waiter over to him, all point to a man with a violent past and probably present. If he has an Eastern European accent, then the most likely diagnosis is that he is…"

"Stop," said Toni, writing on a piece of table napkin; she showed him what she had written – *a professional killer.*

"I was going to say an assassin."

They both looked very serious as they concluded that the red-haired man had come to kill Kovalov!

***

"What can we do?" asked Toni concernedly.

Michael thought for a few moments.

"Pretend we are lovers and kiss me on the lips, then cover for me."

She obeyed and shortly after, Michael got up and staggered past the assassin to the exit, the assassin watching his obviously drunken gait with amused contempt.

Five minutes later, the 'drunk' returned, staggering even more and 'accidentally' lurched into the assassin's table, falling onto his lap. A muscular hand was stuck out and lifted Bullivant into the air.

"You are clumsy man," he said with an Eastern European accent, managing to restrain his other arm from delivering a blow to Bullivant's face.

Toni rushed over, "I am so sorry, so very sorry," she effused, "We have been celebrating our anniversary, and a champagne breakfast in our room and..."

"It's okay, just take him away," he said with a simultaneous smile and snarl.

***

They sat and waited.

"Well, he has finished his coffee, so let's just hope it works," cooed the doctor. "I don't really have a plan B!"

"Did you spike his drink?" she asked, "I didn't see it."

The assassin seemed to become more relaxed, and then his eyes began to droop; he looked like he might fall asleep in the chair but then began to vomit, a terrible uncontrollable vomiting, which caused total chaos in the dining room.

Doctor Bullivant stepped over to the man,

"Oh my God," he shouted, "Get an ambulance – quick 999; I think this poor man has Gilliepeak's Disease."

Explaining that he was a doctor, Michael put the assassin into the recovery position and explained to everyone around that this was a very serious disease spread by parrots in Eastern Europe and it would need immediate hospitalisation. As there was no person-to-person spread there would be no danger to anyone else.

The ambulance came shortly, and though rather surprised by the explanations as they had never heard of the disease before, took the assassin off to the hospital as instructed, where he remained for 12 hours until (furiously) discharging himself.

***

"What did you make of the Kovalov talk?" asked Michael.

"Nothing really… I was watching *you*…but it was very well received anyway. But what did you spike his coffee with?"

"A quick acting sedative and a severe dose of ipecac to induce vomiting from my medical bag in the car; the situation was desperate so I had to use both. The quick-acting sedative would be absorbed before the vomiting started and we would create a medical emergency." He grinned before adding: "And you didn't find your filly, and that is why you are drinking more than you do normally."

"I guess so," she smiled, "and taking advantage of the very generous gentleman who is paying for this expensive meal." She looked more closely at him.

"You're wearing eye shadow!" she started, "and slight rouge…. Ah-"

She stared at him in disbelief.

"-And you are wearing perfume – my favourite." Finally, with great amusement and jollity, she posed the question "Are you trying to seduce me?"

"No, not at all; I am going to let *you* seduce *me*; I will be your substitute filly!"

She smiled at the interesting option handed to her… yes she probably would, and there would be the excitement of not knowing what might happen… he was certainly an interesting man.

***

The next day, breakfast was different from their first breakfast together, as they paid more attention to each other and less to the rest of the diners. The night together had been better than either could have possibly anticipated, rather in the way that a vegetarian meat substitute can sometimes taste better than the real thing.

"But why do you carry sedatives and ipecac?"

"Sedatives in case I really do need a sleep; I would only take a small dose for myself, but the massive dose I prescribed for our assassin friend would work like magic."

"And the ipecac?"

Bullivant looked mysterious.

"Just in case someone tried to poison me." he said.

Toni laughed: "Give me your card, and maybe I will phone you," she said.

"Yes, give me your number, and maybe I will phone you," he replied.

He got up to leave.

"But who would try to poison you?" she asked, looking puzzled.

The doctor looked at the ceiling.

"A jealous lover perhaps," he said, as he minced away from the table, leaving Toni with a broad smile.

The Final Shadow

That strange knotty feeling would soon pass. Funny how the journey down the worm-drain always had that effect. The rest of the journey would be delightful - indeed the VegaTrino star system was universally accepted to be the most awesome sight in Sector 7.

Dempsey stretched his legs and arms and did a minute of Katha Chi; soon the circulation felt better, and his brain was in alpha nine rhythm. His depostles watched patiently; after all, the future of the Accessible Universe rested with their leader, and he had to be in a perfect physical and mental state to meet with the Mnemic.

Comfortable and relaxed on the solar cruiser, Dempsey could review the task ahead... there was much to be done...

***

Through the visuport, he could see the surface of the planet Ultran. He switched off the commentary; you don't come first in your class at Stellar Topography and need that basic stuff. Ultran was the outermost of the VegaTrino planetary system, where the wormport entered its jurisdiction. The blue-white light from Vega stridently shadowed the craters and crevices in the frozen nitrogen mountains against the ultra-white background; by any standards this was beautiful. Far beyond Vega, its companion star Trino threw an even purer blue-white iridescence into space. The planet which lay between the two stars - Eden - was the destination.

As the cruiser lifted from the planet's surface, the sheer size and might of its wildness made the crew gasp. But Dempsey had rehearsed this whole thing so many times in his mind, every image, every sensation, every thought. This was the culmination of his life's work.

Even in the void between the planets, Vega's light was uplifting. How often had he dreamed of being here?

"Your son, Demsey, is unquestionably a genius," his teacher had confided in his parents, "but be warned..." (his parents had frowned and moved closer) "...though you yourselves are golden ones fused in The Heraldics, this genius mind could turn on an electron... he could save the world or destroy it." The teacher stood up and walked away; it was a simple matter of fact.

***

Dempsey smiled at the thoughts of his school days, his humble beginnings and his rise to - well - let's face it - the pinnacle of human achievement. As the leader-designate of Hominid 7 and its protectorates, there could be no greater accolade.

Suddenly a chill broke on his brow, and a shudder went down his spine. What was this feeling? Where was it from? The shadows of the mountains had somehow triggered a strange memory. Perhaps the journey down the wormdrain had disturbed some memories? The early travelers would often call it "The Brain Shaker"... switch that off: focus on the task at hand! The Shadows have no place here.

***

The cruiser moved on to the mid-solar space; the light from both Vega and Trino outshone each other causing the asteroids and their attendant beacons to flicker like giant candles in the luminous void. Planet Eden was as it were - suspended between the two stars. Early astronomers had been unable to conceive of physics that would allow this to happen. But as elsewhere in physics, the facts must create the theory - not vice versa. Indeed Eden's very existence had taken the knowledge of space-time a warpstep forward.

How true also of Dempsey's existence, that reverence for the facts - for the knowledge itself - would take him forward. At school, he was regarded as a hero, as courageous, always willing to take on the impossible. But Dempsey knew that deep-down he was no hero; if you knew the true facts of the case, you need never gamble - and this was Dempsey's true genius. In a conflict, he could always gauge the oppositions' determination, his weaknesses, and where he would eventually yield to the pressure. There were so many ways of knowing the enemy's agenda that Dempsey could never fail.

Another asteroid flickered with a red-green incandescence. A system with no shadows. He shuddered again... The worm-drain had raked up some strange memories, whatever they were, of dream-like terrors. Focus on the job at hand! To be able to focus on the task at hand and dispatch unhelpful thoughts had always been another of Dempsey's awesome attributes.

***

They were passing asteroid 37 - the most frequently depicted sight in the Accessible Universe. Shoulder-to-shoulder, the massive volcanoes eructated their iridescent larva and incandescent ashes into the emerald atmosphere creating a coruscation of lights unique to the known universe. Evanescent shadows raced across the rugged landscape and the light of the twin stars beatified a truly mind-shattering spectacle which immured itself into the consciousness of every observer. (The shudder again at the thought of beautiful shadows chilled Dempsey's neck; he fought it back and expertly re-buried it.)

***

Dempsey's election as leader-designate had been the people's choice and had been sealed by his solemn oath to secure peace with the people of the VegaTrino System. The early people had been stunned to learn that all higher life in the Accessible Universe had come from a common ancestry - that we were all truly brothers and sisters. This realization had astounded and then come to haunt the Earth-Peoples; atrocities perpetrated on members of the same species was indeed a bitter pill to swallow, and the power of this guilt was only exceeded by the fervent desire to make amends. These policy decisions were made easier as they came to learn of the more advanced technical skills of the VegaTrinos, coupled with their immense natural resources which meant they would inevitably surpass earth as a power in the future.

Dempsey's slogan of Reparation, Brotherhood, and Eternal Peace had won the day; it was now his holy mission to deliver on his solemn promise.

***

Dempsey and the depostles donned their light shields; they would only be needed for a few hours until their eyes became accustomed to the luminosity. Stepping down from the cruiser, a most wonderful sight met their eyes - people as far as the eye could see, each one of them waving a blue Suva - the flower of peace. The smell from the flowers enveloped them in a cloud of calmness, optimism, and tranquility.

The traditional journey of welcome lasted a few hours through the cheering crowds. When they took the shields from their eyes, the sight was even more wonderful; these were beautiful happy people... how could we ever have seen them as aliens mused Dempsey. They were somehow like our own hominids 'gone the right way' - almost as though the light from the two suns, the very planetary configurations, were designed to make a hominid more perfect; they were astonishingly beautiful people. Perhaps life had begun here in the very beginning - before the time of the Forgotten Travelers. Perhaps this was where all hominids truly "belonged"; here was certainly paradise.

***

At the Mnemnon, the Mnemic himself was waiting. They bowed low to each and then, to the cheers of the crowd, they exchanged Suva Flowers and embraced each other.

***

Talking with the Mnemic was so easy, and the "deal" had been worked out well in advance so that soon all was sealed and signed. Dempsey had thought long and hard about how the Mnemic would think, what he would need, and what would be acceptable to him. However, the Mnemic was far more intelligent and able to read Dempsey's thoughts than had ever happened before; in many ways, he was like his identical twin from another star.

The wonderful people who helped Dempsey were quite extraordinary. They were relaxed and natural; they seemed to have no unworthy thoughts or feelings: they were beautiful people in every conceivable way. One of the attendants, "Eta" was especially attentive to him and between his talks with the Mnemic he learned so much about her people and their history. The bond grew stronger and stronger, and soon Dempsey knew that something new and extraordinary was happening to him. This did not entirely surprise him, as love had been forbidden to him until he had fulfilled his sacred duties. Now, the power and beauty of his feelings began to overwhelm him, and for the first time he knew true love.

***

"But something still troubles you!"

The Mnemic was as intuitive as Dempsey himself.

"It is Eta," admitted Dempsey immediately and spontaneously, "I cannot bear to think that I must leave this place and never see her again!"

The Mnemic smiled, reached over and embraced Dempsey:

"My son, you have passed the final test. Eta, my beloved daughter is to be your life companion. It has been ordained. She will go with you wherever you will go; she will be the living symbol of the love between our peoples; your love will make our worlds safe."

Tears welled up in the eyes of Dempsey. Yes, his life's work was truly done. Yes, he had found the final love. In this place without shadow, he had found eternal peace and the shadows that had haunted him would never appear again. He passed into a beautiful untroubled sleep.

There was a heavy frost as dawn broke over the Place of Detentions and the chanting of the protesters sent milky clouds into the air.

The governor looked at them with indifference: how, after all, could they be so concerned about so trivial an event as an execution, when hundreds, thousands died every day.

The chanting grew louder. The governor scowled. After all, some people were just too dangerous to be allowed to live. This was not about retribution, but about protecting society from supercriminals – this was the first duty of the state!

The light grew in intensity. It was over now anyway, and the new technologies meant that there would have been no suffering whatsoever. Quite the reverse: the last thoughts of the condemned man before he ceased would be ecstasy and the fulfillment of all his wildest aspirations - everything he had ever hoped for would "happen" for him in the final dream. Yes, the technology called "The Final Shadow" certainly made for the most humane of executions.

The governor moved towards the window and listened to the chanting of the crowds:

"Save Dempsey… Save Dempsey… Save Dempsey…"

The New Recruit

"I'll pay," said George, "it's been a very good term."

Henry accepted the offer, though, as always, felt a little guilty at accepting the generosity of George's ill-gotten gains. Henry rationalised that he was hard up anyway with a wife and child trying to survive in New York – even though he was paid well by the employment agency where he worked.

He often ruminated on the total immorality of George, his exploitation of women in general, and of his students in particular… but he suppressed his moral outrage as George was always very generous with him and the stories of his sexual exploits were riveting.

"And how is your new recruit – your star student?" There was a pause, George looked thoughtful.

"Are you going to fuck her?"

"I have to," said George finally, "I just can't help myself. She is beautiful, has a mind-blowing figure and the way she looks at me with those huge brown Italian eyes… I know she will be an amazing fuck. But some of these foreign girls think they own you after a one-nighter, so I will have to cover my tracks… can I use your place?"

This had happened before; it would happen on the last day of term, before everyone went their separate ways. George was sure it would be easier to cover his tracks and evade pursuit from any broken-hearted 'exploited' girls if they did not know where he lived.

…of course it would be all right.

***

This was the final teaching session of a fantastic year. Even now George had no idea how much money he might make from his students' efforts. In a sense he earned it as he did direct their efforts in his "creative writing course," but then selected the best stories and had them turned into film scripts by his cousin in the mid-west; the results had earned him a fortune and a legendary status under his pen-name of George Recruit.

The 12 students were divided into three groups of four, each with their own remit; the theme was 'The Mediaeval Pilgrim' and each group gave a 15-minute presentation on some aspect of the theme.

Each presentation was superb as would be expected from some of the very best and most creative students around, and even though George had read their research and ideas, he was still totally enthralled by the efforts that these young people made.

As usual, Ariadne was ahead of the pack with her presentation on Disease and its impact on Mediaeval thought. It was so easy for George to turn her hard work into hard cash.

"Where will you go after this term?" he asked her.

"I must go back to my family; I do miss the blue of the Mediterranean and the warm sun… but I will miss you more," she added looking deeply into his eyes. "I don't feel that I have truly got to know my wonderful inspiring teacher."

George smiled and looked at his watch. "Well, you have been the outstanding pupil on my course… and I am free this evening. I almost feel that I owe you dinner – that is if you can keep it a secret?"

The deal was done.

***

Some wine and a reasonable meal in a noisy bar and then an invitation to go back to his place which happened to be 'just around the corner' where they could 'get to know each other better' where there was less noise. Such an easy script to write and just as easy to do.

***

She woke up alone and, with a pang, noticed that he was gone. Something terrifyingly beautiful had happened the night before which had confirmed that George indeed was "the love of her life." By her side on the bed was a red rose and one of George's business cards, and a note which read:

"That was the most beautiful night of my life; I will be in touch soon."

She had a long shower and left the apartment building.

***

Henry was curious: "Well – did you?"

George closed his eyes and shook his head as if in a confessional.

"She was the fuck of the century, Henry; she totally wiped me out!"

He paused.

"I had taken a Viagra to make sure I performed to maximum, but God knows I didn't need it. She was almost like a virgin in her openness to me and let me do anything to her – which I did, of course… the neighbours may well complain about the noise. Oh, my God, she was just a Tsunami of Sex!"

He looked thoughtful and exhausted.

"Will you see her again?" Henry asked.

George laughed.

"Of course not. I left her one of those phoney business cards and a nice note. That's all they get to take away from me – some souvenir, eh?"

George congratulated himself on another conquest, another sexual freebie, and a brilliant erotic memory over which he would masturbate in a slack period.

***

She waited for two days and heard nothing from George. What was she to do? Her flight home left in two weeks but how could she possibly leave New York with this mystery still unsolved? She phoned the number on George's business card but the number was 'decommissioned.' This puzzled her, and she worried that something might have happened to George; in any event, she had to see him again.

There was no address on the business card, but she could remember where they had stayed; yet, when she went to his apartment, a stranger answered who had never heard of George. She was totally baffled, and her mind was in turmoil as to what might have happened. Had he been kidnapped or had a sudden illness? Why had he not been in contact? She sat by the phone waiting for news and as hope began to fade, her tears began to flow…

***

As for George, life carried on as usual – well maybe even a little better than before as he frequently thought of that amazing night of sex and the thrill of 'yet another' conquest.

Then came that fateful night and the authoritative knock at the door.

"Are you George Shapiro?" asked one of the three uniformed men? They stepped in uninvited, and George confirmed that this was indeed George Shapiro. They showed their identification, though with their confident bearing they scarcely needed it; George could tell they were lawmen of some sort.

"We want to ask you some questions, but we are sure you will know what this is all about," said the leader.

"I haven't a notion," said George, "I certainly haven't broken any laws."

The three men looked at each other and laughed.

"We have three complaints of sexual assault and one perhaps even more serious to discuss with you… do you have anything to say at this stage?"

"Nothing," said George. "Are you sure there is not some kind of mistaken identity involved here?"

The men looked at each other and laughed again. "No," said the leader, "None! Before we take you downtown, we just need to check on a couple of things," he added.

Slowly the story unfolded of the three separate allegations. The accounts were interspersed with odd phrases like 'exploitation of your students.' The policemen had no photographs of the women concerned, and George truly could not recollect any of the incidents that were being described. His request for a lawyer was peremptorily dismissed, and when he moved towards the phone, the burliest of the men forcibly sat him down and whispered at him to "not do anything like that again."

To the frustration of the lawmen, George denied everything, even though they advised him strongly to 'co-operate' or things 'would get even worse.'

They told him of the likely consequences of his crimes, as sexual assault had become a "high priority" and prosecutors were particularly eager to secure convictions.

They were preparing to take George downtown for formal charging when George decided to make a stand:

"I am a respectable lecturer," he said with indignation, "and I have a steady girlfriend – why would I need to behave like this? Anyway, I'm sure she will testify that she was with me on those occasions as we spend so much time together." He was clutching at straws, but the situation was totally desperate.

The men looked at each other. "Okay. This could have a bearing on these matters. What's her name?"

George was thinking quickly on his feet:

"She is called Ariadne."

"Let's go meet her," said the leader.

**

Ariadne came to the door in her dressing-gown; she had been crying and did not look great! George sat in the car outside, with one of the policemen for company.

"Is your name Ariadne?" asked the lawman deferentially.

"Yes" answered Ariadne, looking puzzled.

"And do you have a boyfriend called George?"

Ariadne maintained the look of confusion on her face, but inside her mind was racing.

"Yes indeed," she answered with emotion, "is he all right? He isn't hurt is he?"

"No," answered the lawman, "but he is in big trouble. May we bring him in?"

"Of course," answered Ariadne, "but give me five minutes to change; I can't let George see me like this!"

She disappeared into the bathroom and returned 15 minutes later, transformed.

George had been brought into Ariadne's apartment and sat on the sofa. He leaped out of his seat and gave her a genuinely passionate embrace with some whispered tender words in her ear.

"He says he is your boyfriend? Is that so?" asked one of the policemen.

If George were in trouble, then she would certainly rescue the "love of her life" and her creative and nimble mind was racing ahead.

"Absolutely," returned Ariadne. "We have been in love for three months now," she added with a loving smile at George which he readily, and in some trepidation, reciprocated. "In fact," she added with all the creativity of the top student she certainly was, "he proposed marriage to me only the other day, but he had been drinking, and I still don't know if he was serious."

The lawmen looked at George questioningly and in high expectation of the answer:

"Absolutely," said George with both fervour and terror in his voice as he glanced again at the expression on the lawmen's faces, "I truly love her and hope that she will agree to marry me!"

"And what is your answer?" asked the leader with great interest, looking at Ariadne.

"My answer is, of course 'Yes.' I love him with all my heart and always will!"

She looked down at the floor with tears in her eyes for a few moments:

"Unfortunately, I have to return home to Italy in ten days and so, if George agrees then we will have to be married this Saturday so I can take my new husband with me."

The men looked menacingly at George who knew that betraying this beautiful, adoring woman could undo his 'release' from the clutches of the law.

"Of course, Ariadne; it is the only possible thing to do!" he said with a sigh of relief.

The men were clearly very touched by this beautiful girl and wonderful romance they had been privileged to witness.

The leader coughed:

"Well, unfortunately, that may not be possible as there have been some serious allegations against Mr Shapiro, and I am not sure he will be free to travel. However, he claims that on each occasion of these alleged crimes he was with you…"

Ariadne thought for a moment:

"Come with me to the other room, and I'll check the dates in my diary," she said.

***

Ten minutes later, the policeman emerged with Ariadne and with big smiles on their faces. "What a wonderful woman, Mr Shapiro. You are a lucky, lucky bastard!"

He turned to face George.

"It isn't often that me and the boys get to go to a wedding in the line of duty, but I guess Saturday will see you having three extra guests!" He happily slapped George on the back.

The Beast of Satan

The piled logs were covered by a tingling frost that made
them stick to his hands as little Joseph broke them off from
the heap and cradled them in his thin, little arms.

His breath hung like a cloud in the frozen air, and he shivered
in his layers of rags. He quickly hurried back to the hut,
noticing anew the blue wood-smoke and its reassuring smell
as he walked across the clearing.

The mud had frozen hard, into craggy furrows churned over
many times by the pigs' snouting around in the summer.
Now, apart from the breeding pair, the pigs hung salted and
preserved from the roof at the entrance, too high for the
remaining pigs to reach.

They grunted at being disturbed as he pushed his way past
them. The house was warm in the centre where the family
huddled together, crunching into the black bread with their
carious teeth. Grimy faces looked around as he laid the logs
to dry and Joseph's mother moved slowly, pained by her
joints, as she put more wood on the fire. The smoke filled the
room, and the family edged as close to the fire as they dared,
coughing in turn from the choking smoke.

**

Soon it would be Sunday and how much Joseph loved the
church; Heaven itself would be much like the church, so light
with the glass windows, and warm from the packed bodies. It
was the joy of the week to hear the word of God and to hear
the stories of Jesus our Saviour, of his healing of the sick and
the poor, of his great sufferings and of his great love for us.

The priest, Father Matthew, would walk amongst us, give us
his blessing and teach us how to work for our salvation. How
grateful we should all be that the voice of God Himself
should be amongst us. The people sang the hymns of praise
and the air was filled with love. If only he, Joseph, could
someday be a priest or a monk and move closer to this

holiness, this love of God which made all suffering so bearable.

Sometimes, the Lord of the Manor would come and speak. What finery he wore! He, appointed by God to look after us, would speak about the sacrifices we must make to gain paradise. How proud we were when this Lord took our best pig for his own at the Manor! How sometimes he would give out with his own hand the white bread for the people... bread from heaven! These were such good times when the people were together in the love and fear of God.

***

But then, as the years went by, and there was no pestilence, and as the ground gave up bigger crops and the animals became ever more fertile, the people began to complain. No longer did the Sunday Mass fill the church with warm bodies, but people stayed away. Only those with heavy hearts or sickness came for the comfort of Jesus. There were even murmurings against the Lord of the Manor – that man appointed by God to oversee us... these were godless times and God would not permit it: there would be a judgement, and there would be consequences.

***

"Come quick, everyone come quick!" panted little Veronica almost screaming in her alarm. "Come quick, bring pitchforks, bring help, everyone!" she cried desperately pointing into the distance. A group of villagers ran to join her and followed her as she ran. Veronica was a calm child normally; this must be something exceptional. The snow was slippery underfoot, and the villagers struggled to keep pace with the frantic little girl.

"There it is!" she pointed in disbelief. And there was the head of Hercule, the much loved old horse of the Lord of the Manor. There were strange tracks in the snow, a deep furrow and a trail of blood going off into the distance as though some massive creature had ripped off the animal's head and dragged the carcass away.

"We need more help, we need more of us to follow this trail," cried Peter. Three of the group ran back to the village leaving the others staring at the remains of beloved Hercule. What kind of creature could do this thing? It seemed impossible...

They shouted to give each other courage and hopefully to scare off any beast that might be lying in wait. Then, when more villagers arrived, they took courage and told themselves that with so many of them, armed with pitchforks, they could deal with any creature that might be lurking amongst the trees. Into the forest they went and shouted so loudly that showers of snow from the overhanging branches tumbled down. The tracks were easy to follow and, finally, they saw it and the horror of it made them huddle together in the silence of total terror.

The body of the horse had been ripped open and there beside it were the remains of a man... the remains of Columba. His head had been half ripped off and it gaped gruesomely at the villagers like a terrible warning. His clothes had been ripped through, and there was blood everywhere.

The villagers stared in a terrified stillness; the snowed-in forest muffled even their total silence. Then they began to peer in terror around the scene of carnage, lest the beast was seeking another victim. Finally, Peter said:

"The Lord of the Manor must be told; he will protect us and tell us what to do."

***

Then it was like the old days; all the people gathered together in the fear and love of God. Father Matthew conducted an "exceptional Requiem Mass" in which the remains of poor Columba were displayed in a makeshift coffin and prayers were said. The priest reminded us that we all must die someday and answer to our maker; that we must pray night and morning and come to mass each week to make our peace with the Lord God. Columba had drifted away from godliness... he was – more than anyone – the dissenting voice, the non-attender, the one who had strayed from the paths of righteousness which Jesus had laid down for us... the heretic! How each one of us in the congregation was thankful that they had been spared... that they were not like Columba...

***

Father Matthew stood tall amongst his flock. Wherever he went, he was welcomed into their huts with great warmth. Every day he basked in their love, born of fear.

"I believe," he said, "that this was the work of the great Satan and that it was our loss of Faith which allowed this great Satan to come amongst us." He repeated this many times, and his fevered conviction lent power to his words. Every single one of his congregation knew he spoke the truth. Much mead went unconsumed: God had returned to his community.

Even Joseph's prayers took on a new power, and he had never felt so close to God himself; his very terror gave power to his supplications. If only Joseph could be like Father Matthew – a handmaid to the Lord our God. How hard he prayed. Sometimes he felt the words of God inside him, and he prayed that he might someday be like Father Matthew.

These were truly the good times until came the Great Plague which took more than half the village and Father Matthew himself. But by then Joseph was into his religious schooling; his devotion had been noted, and his education at the seminary had been hastened by the needs of the people to have a priest to oversee them.

***

What a joyous return did Joseph make to his village, still scarred and cowed by the ravages of the great plague. He walked among his people, their appointed religious leader, helping them cope with the pain and sufferings of their lives and bringing them closer to Jesus and their God.

These, too, were good times; the church was packed every Sunday and Joseph reminded all the flock of the "Beast of Satan" which could strike at any moment should they stray from the path of righteousness.

**

But then came more fertile years when everything thrived. There were bumper crops, and the herds became bigger than anyone could remember; even the winters did not seem so severe. These were times of plenty. Yet to Joseph these were times of the Devil. His sermons remained as passionate as ever, but now he spoke to an ever-dwindling flock. He even heard rumours of heretical talk in the village. How could the people be so blind and stupid? How could they turn their backs on the Lord, our God? And how could he, Joseph, bring his people back to the paths of righteousness? Surely in his Heaven, Jesus could see what needed to be done? He had unleashed the Beast of Satan upon a wavering village before, so surely now he would do it again?

**

"Bless me, Father, for I have sinned. It is now 15 years since my last confession."

Father Joseph did not recognise the voice, nor could he see the figure through the grille. It was rare to have a total stranger at his church.

"May God forgive me father, for I have been a wicked man. I have committed adultery and many sins of lechery. I have been drunken and gluttonous. I have stolen many goods... but above all Father," he whispered, "I have murdered a man."

The church was empty and the silence echoed around its walls.

"What I will add, Father, is that I must now make my peace with the Lord. From now on, Holy Father, I will devote my life to Jesus and become worthy of the clothes that I wear. Never, ever, will I commit sins like these again, for blood and death have brought me to my senses and back to Jesus our God and Lord."

Father Joseph felt a cold shudder go down his spine; he had never heard the confession of a murderer.

"Which man did you kill and for what reason?" he asked.

"I was paid to kill a stranger who I now know was called Columba."

Father Joseph's mouth became dry, and his heart pounded in his chest: was this man before him the true Beast of Satan?

"And I was paid well to do this brutal deed, and so before our Holy Father I must bear the guilt and shame of what I did."

"And who paid you?" asked the priest, controlling the tremble in his voice.

"Let me say, dear Father, that there was an old, useless horse whose death was not far away and his owner had me kill him and also the villain Columba. It was a worthy deed, and had I done it in the name of God, it was no crime. But I took the money and the guilt."

Joseph took a deep breath and with the solemnity of his office said:

"And now, my son, do you foreswear of all such deeds in the future?"

"Father, I swear on all that is sacred, by the blood of the saints that never will I enter into those sins again. Now that such horrors have awakened me into the love of Jesus, my life is renewed."

Father Joseph solemnly blessed the sinner and by the power of God forgave him his sins. There was penance to pay, but he could begin a new man.

Yet... could he have done these deeds alone? Could one man have dragged a horse through the snow by himself?

Father Joseph finished his prayers of absolution. The penitent stood up and moved from the confessional. Father Joseph peered out and saw a huge figure in a monk's robe stepping out of the church... eerily in the candlelight, the absolved man looked like a giant.

***

Father Joseph was a good man who truly loved his flock. How could he bring them back to the fear and love of God? His hope that the Beast would return was now shattered and the godlessness in his village would just fester and grow as they moved away from Jesus. In his dealings with the Lord of the Manor, Joseph hid his feelings, mixed as they were with fear and shame. He was now bound forever to such a ruthless and evil ally, yet a man who in past times he would have gladly confided in. Anyhow, this same Lord was becoming old, and his involvement in recruitment for the foreign wars meant that he had lost interest in the village.

Father Joseph stood alone; a solitary soul facing a tide of evil. How he prayed; how he fasted. His eyes took on a wild look, and the passion in his sermons seemed to fall on stony ground and even to drive more of his flock away. His hunger remained to do the work of God, to save the souls of his flock. Yet how? He knew that the hand of God could strike in different ways, and he truly did not know how it might happen.

Was the murder of Hercule and Columba an indirect act of God Himself? Surely God who knew all things would send another sign?

***

Then he began to pray in earnest for the return of the Beast of Satan. At first, his prayers were cautious; he was unsure whether this was a worthy request. But then he seemed to hear the voice of God saying that such prayers were acceptable and that the people must be made to see the folly of their ways. He fasted, he prayed, he hoped… he began to expect.

***

"Father Joseph, Father Joseph, come quick, come quick."

The child was hysterical.

"What is it, my child?" asked the priest.

"The Beast, the Beast has come down upon us again."

The child's eyes were wild with terror and even in the distance, he could hear the cries of the villagers. The legend of the Beast was taught in the church and often told to the children in their huts; each of them knew that the Beast could return at any time.

"Give me one minute to find my cloak," said the priest with a grim smile; his prayers had been answered.

He stepped into the vestry and threw on his cloak, pausing just a moment to wipe the remains of the fresh blood from the huge brass crucifix which had been used in the service of God.

He stepped out to reclaim his flock for Jesus.

Armando Aguilla: Chief of Police

The committee let out a collective groan. There had been no external application for the newly-vacated job of police chief; they would have to appoint from within the department.

"What about Jose Nabarro?" asked Maria, the only female on the committee, "He is a possible candidate, though I must admit that he is my godson."

The four other members stared in disbelief, their mouths agape. Paulo, the chairman, shook his head and politely and patiently pointed out that he had taken at least one bribe and was still under scrutiny.

"Fernando Wonchoppe?" suggested Franco with a look of hopeless desperation.

Paulo sighed: "Thanks but no! He has dried out just now, but he does have a severe drink problem, and I needn't remind this committee about the fire engine and the school roof affair." They all grunted in total agreement; that incident had been very unpleasant and was imprinted on all their memories.

"Antonio? Antonio Mescalto?" suggested Bernardo despairingly.

Paulo shook his head in dejection.

"He is a womaniser – always in trouble with the fairer (and sometimes) uglier sex." They all laughed: they were only too aware of the sometimes bizarre sexual aberrations of Antonio Mescalto.

Several other names were suggested; each one was given without any attempt to hide the desperation which all of the committee felt. In fact, there was only one possible choice, and deep down they all knew it. It had to be "the Virgin" - Armando Aguilla!

"But he is too dull to be even a lighthouse keeper," intoned Bernardo. "I got stuck talking to him outside church once. I swear that he spoke for a whole hour on the life and legends of Saint Christopher! I was going crazy! I had to pretend I had an attack of diarrhoea to get away!"

"Yes, yes, but let us remember that he has never had any blemishes on his career and does things exactly by the book."

They all nodded. That was certainly true.

"He once cornered me and wouldn't stop talking about omelettes and all the different ways of making them: I wanted to die!" added Franco.

They all had similar stories to tell about Armando Aguilla, but truly there was no other choice. Armando "the Virgin" Aguilla would be the next Chief of Police.

***

"Great news, my dear mother, you had better sit down for this. I, Armando Aguilla, have been made Chief of Police!" He had rushed out after the announcement to let his dear mother be the first to receive the good news. She was truly amazed and thanked him for phoning her; unfortunately, she had to rush off to a "hairdressing appointment," or she might have spoken for a little longer (The truth was that she would rather talk to the cat than her boring son.)

"Yes!" said Armando, clenching his fist. "This is the greatest day of my life!"

He made his way to the jewellery store. He would buy the engagement ring and go straight away to propose to his beloved Isabella. He knew her size perfectly – her ring finger was the same size as his little finger – they had tested it when they had spoken about getting engaged some seven years earlier. The salesmen seemed to be avoiding him at first, until he eventually cornered one.

"Ah, Signor Aguilla," he said, facing a likely protracted and very small-value sale, "How can I help you?"

***

Two hours later, Armando walked out clutching the ring. It would be a perfect fit and what a fabulous ring at such a good price; there were three "holes" where further gems could be added in the future, but the beautiful central topaz quite bedazzled the proud Armando. The salesman was extremely happy with the deal, amazed that he had managed to sell the second-hand ring with missing gems at all; additionally, he had sold Armando the large tube of (expensive) "jeweller's glue" so that in the future he could set in gems which he and his beloved Isabella could purchase together.

**

Armando rarely went near her house, and his heart beat wildly in his chest as he approached it. In spite of escorting her to mass every Sunday and, of course, the annual Christmas party at the police department, he had never entered her home.

He rapped on the door with all the masculine authority of a man who had come to claim his well-earned prize.

"Who is that?" cried the startled voice from within.

"It is your faithful friend Armando who has been made Chief of Police and requests that you become engaged to be married!" he announced confidently.

"Who is that?" asked a bored male voice from inside. Armando heard her whispering something, and she came to the door in her dressing gown.

"You have been made Chief of Police?" she asked incredulously.

"Yes indeed!" said the proud policeman, "and I have brought you this beautiful engagement ring so that we can be engaged to be married!"

Isabella was dumbfounded, and her dressing gown fell open. Armando did not even notice her exposed breast, but proudly showed her the ring. She looked at it even more dumbfounded.

"Well. Will you marry me?" he asked with no doubt whatsoever that the answer would be in the affirmative.

"Tell him to fuck off and come back to bed," came a drunken male voice from the interior.

There was a stunned silence. Isabella just stared into space; Armando, noticing her dressing gown had fallen open pulled the opening shut and knotted the belt.

"I... that is he is... pregnant and boyfriend... and I... unexpected... I must..."

A large semi-naked man thrust himself in front of her, and in a slurred, threatening voice, with vigorous pointing gestures advised Armando as to what should be his next course of action.

"My woman!" he said pointing at her, "Pregnant! You fuck off!"

Armando, stunned and immobile like a statue, with mouth agape, took a while to adjust to these new and startling developments; then, finally with a long and despairing look at his beloved asked:

"Is that your final answer?"

***

From being the best day of his life, this had turned unquestionably into being the worst, and as always when life threw him some unexpected problems, Armando went to his church. First, he went to St Anthony's altar, for here was the patron saint of lost causes! However, in his heart, he knew that even St Anthony could not rescue this situation, so he knelt below the crucifix and prayed to his God. Life was over for him; his dream of marrying the beautiful (well, perhaps "cuddly" might be more exact) Isabella was gone; all his hopes and dreams of marriage and family lay in tatters. He prayed to God to end his life, for death by his own hand would be a mortal sin and with his mind in such turmoil he was desperate to hear some words of solace from Heaven.

Then, something happened that would change his life forever; he thought he heard the voice of Jesus inside his own head and his Holy Master spoke thus:

'Do not despair my son, but follow the path of righteousness and if death should come to you in Love's Service, the doors of Paradise will be opened unto thee.' Armando was startled and prayed awhile in silence, digesting the words of the Lord. Finally, he walked out of church, the burden taken from his shoulders; now he knew what he must do!

***

The previous Police Chief had been a very moral man and had tried to stamp out any illegal activity in the town, including every conceivable motoring offence, prostitution, alcohol distillation and many other 'traditional' activities which had led to him being very unpopular with the general public. The criminal fraternity had been especially furious at their loss of earnings, and his unexpected 'retirement' was rumoured to have been precipitated by some credible threats to his life and possessions. Most of the townsfolk secretly applauded this act of 'persuasion' especially as outsider criminals were trying to move in with drugs and even worse activities. In fact, and, with some tacit public 'approval,' the gangs had declared a certain red light district a no go area and threatened to shoot and kill any policeman entering it.

To Armando, this was a disgrace, and the problem had to be resolved; he looked around at his 'team.'

"What we need is a decoy," he said, "with full backup, so that after the first shot has been fired the whole team moves in, removes the gunman or gunmen and opens up the area once more to normal policing." They all agreed, but then looked away; there were going to be no volunteers for this particular mission. There was a tense silence.

"…and I will be the decoy," said the new Police Chief, matter-of-factly. There were lots of "buts" and objections, but basically, it was better to be Armando than any of them!

"Operation Clear-up" was scheduled for the next evening. Delays would be pointless and possibly risky as there had been rumours of leaks from the department. Armando had just one last thing to do; to make his final confession.

***

So that evening he called in at his church, resolving to explain everything and receive absolution of his sins so that he would enter Heaven in a perfect state of grace. He told the priest about his promotion, about Isabella, and his devotion to St Christopher and how he needed to clean up the town and even though it would be risking his own life, in the service of love it was totally justified.

"… so Father, this will probably be my last confession as I face death alone and unafraid."

The courageous Chief of Police had been quite moved by his account of his impending death and had not noticed the steady, rather sonorous breathing of the priest.

"So please Father, give me absolution so that I may face death with a stainless soul." There was silence (apart from the steady breathing of the priest), "Father, Father, are you there?" he asked raising his voice. The priest started.

"Will you give me your blessing on this venture and absolve me of my sins so that I may enter Paradise in a state of grace?"

"Oh yes, yes indeed," declared the priest, thankful for a final escape.

There was, by now, a queue of people waiting to go to confession and when they saw who had been holding them up for the last 45 minutes there was some amazement… perhaps there was more to "The Virgin" than they had realised.

That night Armando Aguilla slept soundly, knowing that the offer of Paradise was certain and that tomorrow would be his last day on this earth.

***

He began to walk up the hill, with a light heart, knowing that soon all his pain would be gone. He had instructed the nest of armed police to await his orders before they moved in and, of course, he had no intention of calling them in. He had switched off the walkie-talkie.

The red-light district was almost like a fortress as indeed it had been in the early days of Spanish occupation. He noticed the sound of his steps on the ancient stones, the beautiful blue ocean in the distance and the imposing citadel up ahead. Finally, a shot rang out and nearly deafened him. At first, he thought he had been hit, but the bullet had ricocheted off the wall just by his left arm. He continued to walk on. Another shot rang out - and that one missed too! He began to walk in the middle of the street to make himself an easier target. It was clear where the shot had come from, and he ended up after two more near-misses just walking right on into the building.

"Are you drunk?" he yelled at the young man behind the rifle. He was furious with him for depriving him of his journey into Paradise. He grabbed him, took the rifle away from him and slapped him several times across the face in sheer frustration. The young man pointed to a package and some equipment; he had been taking heroin – that is why the idiot had missed. Armando sat down wondering what on earth to do next; he certainly hadn't anticipated this turn of events.

Then came a barrage of gunfire, some he recognised as police guns in the distance but others from quite close.

Finally, a band of about five men burst into the room.

"Keep them pinned down," said a weary, sweaty old man.

He pointed a gun at Armando's head.

"And who, in the name of the Virgin Mary, are you?"

"I am Armando Aguilla, Chief of Police," was the reply, hoping that this might lead to the pulling of the trigger.

"Yes, and I am Napoleon Bonaparte," sneered the old man. "Sit down with your hands on your head!"

He took out his mobile phone and made a frantic call, much of which Armando could not follow, but it was full of expletives and incredulities.

He finally put down the phone and the gun and smiled. "Forgive me, Signor," he said, "but I must search you."

All he found was the switched off walkie-talkie.

"You come here with no gun, no body armour and a switched off walkie-talkie! If my son had not been so stoned off his head on this shit, you would now be dead, mon amigo!"

"You should be ashamed to have a son who abuses drugs!" said the Police Chief with unusual passion. He had not only seen some of the consequences of drugs but had seen a lot of American movies about them and firmly believed that they were the work of the devil himself!

Suddenly the gangster's face softened. He smiled and stretched out his hand.

"My name is Don Juan of Castilla. Please speak to your men on your walkie talkie – call them off. I think we can do business."

***

"I tried to be a good father, but I had to be away a lot and..." explained the old man with tears in his eyes, "...his mother gave him too much money, too much freedom. Sometimes women make bad decisions when left to themselves, don't you think so amigo?"

He looked quizzically at the policeman. In the light of recent events, Armando agreed most definitely!

Now, when you have narrowly missed death – even though it was planned – a few drinks of whiskey with a friendly, wise old man were very welcome, and they were soon talking about the evils of drugs which they both seemed to detest

44

with equal passion. They spoke about women, about the value of arranged marriage, which for the moment at least seemed to appeal to both men. Of course, women should be allowed to make money, but they do need protection. There seemed to be no point on which they disagreed. This was the nicest conversation that Armando had ever had; they even seemed to have the same favourite saint (Saint Christopher) and have an enthusiasm for omelettes.

Finally, the deal was struck, and Don Juan gave the seal of the deal in the form of three small diamonds. For safety, Armando stuck them into the ring with the special glue, both of which he still had in his left trouser pocket.

***

Armando "the Virgin" Aguilla made a strange sight, walking down the hill, pushing a cart loaded with guns and drugs.

His powerful friend on the hill would fight drugs "with everything at his disposal" and would tip off the Police Chief by using the code "Armadillo" for important messages.

By the time he arrived at the bottom of the hill, there was a crowd of police, reporters, and passers-by, and, initiated by the police, they burst into an astonished round of applause at such a daring outcome. Then, overcome by the heat, the drink, and the excitement, Armando Aquila passed into a dead faint.

***

The papers were full of the story. The new police chief, now known as "The Eagle" had become a hero overnight. Of course, he could not tell the story with complete truth – that this had been an aborted suicide mission – and so he had been forced to change a few details. In fact, the only excuse he could come up with for going alone up the hill was:

"I would never ask one of my men to do anything that I would not do myself!" Even at work, "the Virgin" had become an object of respect and enquiries about joining the police department increased considerably!

He still prayed every day at the church and had re-affirmation from his God that the gates of Paradise would be waiting, but how was he to meet his death 'in the line of duty?'

He always wore his police uniform, in the hope that this would make him a more recognisable target; in fact, he would run along the beach "improving police fitness" wearing his distinctive clothes of office in the hope of being shot by some police-hating sniper. He still grieved for his beloved Isabella and as often happens, lost some weight in that grieving. He improved his various police skills, hoping that they might provide a further reason for him to go into whatever danger zones there might be and thus make his escape from his wretched life here on earth.

Yet "The Eagle" became more popular every day. Everywhere he went, people waved to him, and when he went around the red-light district, so many beautiful young women waved at him from their windows. The local paper ran a story on him entitled "The most eligible bachelor in the country?"

There had been not one attempt on his life – not one! This may or may not have been related to the protection order put on him by Don Juan of Castilla, but for whatever reason, these were very good times – apart from the fact that he was determined to have his miserable life ended!

***

"It is someone for you, Chief. He says he is the Armadillo and must speak to you personally."

Armando started; this might be his big chance.

"Tomorrow night, between 10 and midnight, coming over the border from Stella Madre, a big drug consignment in a green van with "Mason's Confectioners" written on the side. They will be heavily armed. I beg you, dear friend, do not go there yourself - promise me."

"I must be there," said The Eagle, overjoyed, "I am the Chief of Police. Is that my dear friend Don…?" but the phone was already dead.

***

His men by now had accepted his total unorthodoxy. To appease them he had taken a gun, and they had helped him set up a barrier across the road which could be raised or lowered. He instructed a handful of them to wait a mile further down the mountain-side 'in the unlikely event' of him not being able to handle the situation himself.

He waited. It was a clear and silent night. He felt that this was his true destiny, to die in the line of duty, fighting drug-trafficking. In just a few hours he would be at the gates of paradise.

First, he heard the van in the distance – maybe several miles away. Then there was a bang – was it an explosion? Then there was some shouting and a few rounds of gunfire. Then more shouting and swearing. Then silence. Silence that lasted for maybe 45 minutes and was finally broken as the engine started up again. He stood in front of the barrier to await his fate.

***

He heard the van moving slowly down the hill, closer and closer. When he flagged it down, it stopped obediently, and a young and beautiful – no, truly very beautiful - young woman stepped out.

"I am Police Chief Armando Aguilla," he announced. "Please be seated while I inspect the contents of your van." The poor young woman looked terrified and sat down obediently. In the back of the van, four men were heavily bound and gagged; their frightening array of guns laid on top of what appeared to be the 'consignment.' He shut and locked the door. Again death had been denied to him. He beckoned the woman to the passenger seat and drove down the hill. He reassured himself that, as Police Chief, he was insured to drive any vehicle.

***

Back at headquarters, the entire police department celebrated. The gangsters found bound and gagged in the back were saying nothing, but they could each be identified as "most wanted criminals," and all that needed to be done was to keep them secure in separate cells until they could be transported on.

This latest story of "The Eagle" had taken Armando Aguilla to further legendary status, and his responses to the amazed "How did you do all this?" questions made him an even greater hero. "I did nothing – just my duty," was his simple and truthful answer.

The key to the whole story was the young woman. She was clearly some kind of accessory to the whole thing but spoke a strange dialect which was hard to understand. Armando wanted to sort the whole thing out that very evening. Sadly all the prison cells were occupied by the arrested men, and there was nowhere to put his key witness.

"I will continue the interrogation at my own home," announced the Eagle. "I have studied dialects, and in her current state of mind I know she will tell me the complete truth." The sniggers that may have started in the nasal passages of the policemen were quickly extinguished. The Eagle was a religious man of the utmost integrity.

***

And it did take the whole night to unravel what had happened. Apparently, "Carolina" had been hired by some men to drive the van, and her father had given permission after the offer of a significant amount of cash. Presumably, a woman driving a van would not have aroused so much suspicion. Then they had developed a flat tyre and been surrounded by unknown gunmen who had tied up her companions, changed the wheel, and instructed her to drive slowly down the mountain.

How Armando's heart melted for the brave young woman; she had obeyed her father and astonishingly had a Saint Christopher's medal around her neck. She helped him to write the report.

He was elated and exhausted. She began to weep.

"Why do you weep, Carolina?" asked the happy policeman. Well, she explained, it had been a long day and she had been so frightened and this was the first day she had spent away from her family, and would he please put his arm around her, like her father did for protection. How she enjoyed the omelette he made and the "special occasion" wine he brought out to celebrate the success of his mission. He felt a gushing of joy for this beautiful, brave creature who seemed to share so many of his views and interests. "Hold me tighter, please dear Armando," she said. "I have been so afraid."

***

Who knows what was most to blame? The excitement of the day, the wine, the loneliness of the two lost souls, but Armando Aguilla could no longer, in reality, be called "The Virgin" having been swept along by a tide just a strong as – and maybe even part of – his deep love of Jesus. In the aftershock of the most profound experience he could ever remember, they joined hands and prayed to St Christopher, asked Jesus for forgiveness, and then got "swept along" two times more.

Armando Aguilla was profoundly monogamistic, and for him it was clear what had to happen next; he produced the ring – now with a full set of gems of course – and proposed that they legalise their union. Carolina was too stunned to refuse his offer of marriage – not that she would have wanted to anyway; the experience had been totally overwhelming for her too, and she had a deep sense of fate about how things usually happen for the best.

The wedding, just one month after that fateful night, was the biggest event the police department – and in truth, the whole town – had experienced in a decade. Everyone went – even Armando's mother – and the newspaper was full of photographs and wonderful things to say about the couple.

"The Eagle" who became known as "The Father of Modern Policing" for his integrity, his pragmatism, the devotion of his men, and his courage, became a true legend and inspired a dynasty in the area. He and Carolina had three sons who all followed in their father's footsteps and two daughters who tried to do the same, but whose beauty soon had them married to policemen themselves. In retrospect, of course, it had been the fateful night of the "interrogation" which had been the start of that magnificent era which served their people so well, although it was probably more than fortunate that no-one saw the look that passed between Carolina and Don Juan, and that intimate, friendly wink that foretold the glorious future.

The Storm

Dawn quietly slipped between the blocks and, totally at home in her diving gear, continued her inspection of their undersurfaces. Even directly beneath them, there was plenty of light to see the rainbows of fishes swarming in the sheltered warmth.

Each block was checked every week, not just by a 'young worker' such as Dawn, but also by an experienced Elder: their whole survival depended on maintaining the floating island to perfection. It was obsessive, and it had to be, but it was also very good discipline for all the Brethren to have a shared vigilance.

Dawn swam on and ran her hands through the layers of rich sea-weed; how could so crude a plant be made into such delicious food she wondered to herself. All was well with this section. She climbed out and took off the diving gear. The blocks at this periphery swayed on the water, though they would soon be made into 'terra firma' by the engineers. She moved leisurely.

The gentle Pacific breeze, the blue sky, the mewing of the seabirds: everything felt so wonderful, and the distant throb of the radon motors which slowly moved the floating island to safer sectors felt so reassuring. They were taught to say out loud four times a day "There is nowhere I would rather be; there is nothing I would rather be doing,"... no rush no irrelevant thoughts, just the glorious present.

Soon, Dawn was on terra firma, and she sniffed the air for the perfumes from their man-made flower-orchards. She wandered between the shrubs, noticing the glorious butterflies, the sounds of the birds, and the exquisite colours of the flowers. This truly was paradise.

And it would remain so for 184 years – in statistical probability terms. The Brethren all knew that statistics could not accurately predict the random play of chance, but the "catastrophe" which would inevitably destroy all the Brethren

– all 25,243 of them – would statistically not strike until then. Of course, it could be any time, or might be deferred for even longer; there might even be some "unforeseeable" happenings that might send all predictions awry, but statistically, the allotted time was 184 years. Dawn rarely even thought about it. She might be dead by then. Her own children – if she had any children – would have died by then; such thoughts were totally "unhelpful."

***

She wandered by the coconut palms and looked across the freshwater lake – beautiful and pale green with a small island where the turtles lived.

She heard some laughter coming from a small coconut palm hut. She listened from outside; her friends were talking happily about their encounter with the friendly whale and how they had ridden on its back. She sipped on fruit juice and enjoyed the rainbow in the fine spray from the cooling fountain. Each child was physically perfect: perfect teeth, perfect weight, perfect hair, and perfect sun-bronzed skin. Each child was psychologically perfected by the upbringing ordained by the elders. This was necessary, as each member of the community needed to be a team member, to help each other, and to know that death was inevitable and their whole community would someday be wiped out... statistically in 184 years.

***

When Dawn had 'become of age' and she was allowed – and indeed, encouraged – to experience 'the Union,' she singled out her handsome friend Thomas and made her request. He had taken her to the Western edge at sunset as she had asked; he had held her hand and then put his hand around her waist; how beautiful this had seemed - to be close to such a handsome male member of the Brethren. She felt a thrill and a shiver as he touched and enjoyed her breasts and then to pleasure her femaleness, first with his hands and then with his maleness. This had, of course, been her first time and she had not experienced "The Big Pleasure" which was her entitlement. They lay in each other's arms, with a strange mixture of togetherness (which she loved) and yet some disappointment.

"I must take you to see a Union Master so that you can have The Great Pleasure," explained Thomas.

Dawn accepted obediently; the rules must be obeyed.

***

The next day, they went to see a Union Master in his pavilion; Thomas was encouraged to watch so that he would know better how to deliver The Great Pleasure to any female who would request him.

In the semi-darkness, the Master laid Dawn out on the soft 'love-bed' which felt so relaxing against her skin. There were strange, relaxing sounds in the background and aromas she had never experienced before. The Master bade her lie on her front and began to massage her back with first gentle strokes, then deeper and deeper ones; she felt at one with the Master's hands as they probed deeper.

He turned her onto her back and gently moved from the gentle skin strokes to the deeper more personal touches. She noticed that she was feeling flushed and breathing more rapidly as he moved his head onto her femaleness and began to give her The Lover's Kiss. She heard herself cry out as she felt The Great Pleasure for the first time. After a while, he continued and took her higher again until she sighed into another Great Pleasure. She felt that she had to have his manhood inside her and he chose the perfect moment; then she had the noisiest and biggest of the Great Pleasures and relaxed into a blissful sleep.

Yet, although this had been a great pleasure for Dawn, she had not been anxious to repeat any of it, which puzzled her. Indeed, she reduced her contact with her friends in case she should be asked to make the union; it was regarded as 'highly desirable' that all such requests should be honoured as sexual frustration in the religious and more primitive societies had been associated with violence and antisocial behaviour. Dawn felt strangely alone…

***

Once, every week, the family had an evening meal together; this was advised by the elders and was a chance to talk about family matters and bond the smaller units together for "K-type emergencies."

Around the table were her two younger sisters and the baby brother; she told them of her swims in the 'shallows' and of her drink by the fountain. The younger sisters spoke of school and their new teacher. The atmosphere was so happy – like always – well, nearly always: just once each year the community was 'advised' (no-one ever disobeyed an "advice") to watch a news update from the "False World" – a reminder of the peoples that lived on the land continents and the miseries that they were forced to endure.

The distress that everyone felt after watching these 'updates' was reflected on everyone's faces for weeks after the showing, but gradually, like now, they learned to forget the "outside world" as though it never existed. After all, the whole purpose of the Sea Brethren was to escape from the False World.

At the end of the meal, Mother raised her hand for their attention. "Children," she began, "I must inform you of something significant to our family unit. Today I have seen the doctors, and they have informed me that I have (statistically) just 147 days left to live. I have a cancer which will kill me. The best treatment will allow me to live this length of time with a possibility of 10 days either way. I have just a 1 in 3 chance of having severe pain and a 2 in 3 chance of feeling so ill that I may accept the death drink before that time, but the 147 days has factored in all of these possibilities, including the state of my immune system."

The youngest of the daughters looked at her mother and her lip began to tremble.

"Stand up small one!" ordered her mother, "Don't you remember what we are taught by the elders? 'There is nowhere I would rather be; there is nothing I would rather be doing!' The feelings you show now are from the False World. We must all die some day and I will just die a little sooner. The Brethren must always live with death as their permanent companion with no fear and no regret... you will learn as you grow older. Control your feelings, or I must enrol you in the emotional re-education class."

The little girl took a deep breath and bit on her lip.

"There is another item I must share," she continued. "Because my life is now valued at a lower level – at 74 units, I have been assigned to sector 6 for the forthcoming storm."

The children nodded resignedly. Everyone was informed of forthcoming storms and their statistical dangers. The current one was certain to hit sector 6 in 2.4 days with a statistical chance of 0.6 to 1.1 deaths. In a storm, it was essential to have "Report and Repair" detachments and generally it was those with less value to the community who were assigned to the more dangerous zones.

"I will be assigned with you, Mother, to Report and Repair in sector 6," said Dawn.

Mother's face clouded over with a mixture of astonishment and disappointment.

"That is a ridiculous idea," she chided roughly. "Your unit value is over 500, and your loss to the community is unthinkable... just read the book of the elders once more and think fitting thoughts!"

***

Mother had never been so close to a real storm before; it was like the anger of the heavens had unleashed all its hatred and fury on sector 6. The blocks rose and fell and fountains of water rushed between them. Ropes and crampon shoes held her safe and her slow movements allowed her to check any damaged ties between the new blocks. The noise of the thunder and the sea conspired to create a deafening duet.

Twice the blocks opened beneath her and she sunk deep into the ocean, but the blocks were light and dragged her back to the surface, leaving her gasping. She was prepared for death; she had been properly educated. She thought of Dawn; she too must be properly taught.

A huge sector of blocks snapped off and flew into the air. To be hit by one of these was certain death yet, with no fear of death, the storm was exhilarating, a sharing of the ocean's power. Again, the blocks parted, and a spout of ocean shot her up into the air. Mother laughed aloud through her choking, "Death, you have no power over me!" she cried in happy defiance.

The storm cleared as quickly as it had come. The reassuring distant drum of the radon motors continued. Mother felt truly alive.

***

The sky lightened for a new day; all was well, and the whole island seemed more tranquil from surviving the violence of the storm. As Mother approached her home-hut, she noticed a figure sitting outside.

Dawn saw her and rushed towards her with her outstretched arms.

"Mother!" she cried in joy with tears in her eyes.

Mother embraced her daughter and felt the hot tingle of tears welling up in her own.

"Dawn... you must study the books of the elders more carefully," she said.

***

Mother decided that she should refer Dawn to the elders for emotional re-education; sentiments like hers would be a danger to her and others. In this community, there was no place for tears - such emotions must be extinguished at all times. She herself must re-enrol also; the storm had exposed some family weaknesses!

The storm had also done some serious damage elsewhere. Although the scientific elders were wise, their predictions were sometimes in error; the storm had turned unexpectedly into sector A4 and swallowed up one of the radon stockpiles. The tragedy of this was not immediately apparent to the Brethren, but the loss of fuel for the radon motors clearly would reduce their ability to move their island so effectively in the future; the net effect would be a loss of survival prospect for the Brethren of 74.7 years… a major disaster in the greater scheme of things.

***

Dawn was on "Periphery Camp." She had been assigned the tasks of monitoring, repairing, and sample-taking in New Sector 73B. She was swimming alone under the blocks, taking samples of various molluscs adherent to their undersides, and putting them in their containers from her backpack. It was idyllic! The beautiful blue water seemed to be rejoicing and the fish, unafraid, played on her skin. A place of total harmony. Then she saw it! At first, it looked like a huge dead turtle floating, motionless. This would need to be reported immediately in case it carried any disease that could affect the Brethren – it should not be touched or sampled. She circled the carcass. Then she realised it was human! She circled around it, her heart pounding. Then she saw something else; she saw a hand move… almost as though it were asking for help.

In the heat of the moment, Dawn forgot the first and most important commandment of the Brethren: "Never approach an alien being." This law was set in stone as contact with an alien could bring new diseases to the Brethren and could even wipe out the entire community. Dawn knew deep down that such behaviour inevitably called down the final punishment, but she was already pulling the limp body up onto the blocks.

The Brethren were fit and strong and even with a body weighing more than herself, Dawn managed to grapple it out of the water. She pushed on its back, water came from its mouth, and after what seemed like ages, it began to choke and cough. Dawn brought some water from her pack and held it to the lips of this golden boy. He sipped and choked a little, then his eyes opened and he moved.

Dawn startled back, but the Golden Boy was too weak to move.

She sat and stared at the beautiful creature before her; to Dawn he looked like an Angel. As he slept, Dawn hurried to the children's camp to get some food – he must surely be hungry after all his traumas. She avoided the others, thinking it best that they did not get involved in such an illegal undertaking; yet surely she could not let the Golden Boy die?

He awoke and rubbed his eyes and smiled at her. After a few moments, he made movements towards his mouth with an enquiring look on his face, and Dawn responded by handing him some fruit. For perhaps an hour they communicated with noises and signs, for their cultures had drifted far apart over the years.

Then, above the drone of the Radon motors, came another sound – a different engine sound which came nearer and nearer. They looked up and, there, now low in the sky was a turbocopter. It came close and hovered above the sea just a short swim away.

The Golden Boy shrugged his shoulders and opened his hands as if in apology. He swiftly jumped into the sea and swam towards the turbocopter which had now alighted on the water.

He climbed aboard gave a final wave and was gone.

***

Then coming in from the next sector, Dawn saw an unusual creature moving in her direction.

"It is Sharkskin!" she said matter-of-factly to herself and indeed it was.

She knew immediately what it meant. The sharkskin suit was worn to protect Brethren from infection and contamination when there was danger.

"Yes, they must have found out about the Golden Boy and the Brethren must be kept safe at all times," Dawn mused to herself.

The Sharkskin raised some kind of weapon and pointed it at Dawn, who sat unemotional, accepting her death with trained equanimity. The deed was done – quickly and unemotionally as per the training manual.

The Sharkskin placed the young body into the incinerator bin and moved quickly through decontamination, the operator knowing that she had done the only possible thing to protect the Brethren. Yet she found satisfaction in her deed hard to find. Had her daughter, Dawn, known that it was her own mother in the Sharkskin? Mother thought that she had seen a look of recognition in her daughter's eyes, but maybe it was just her imagination.

Mother felt weary; now there was just emptiness, and for the first time, tears began to pour down her cheeks. She got into the water and swam; she swam and swam until her limbs became weary, then she swam some more. She continued out to sea until the island disappeared into the distance. She swam until her body gave up, her breathing stopped, and the ocean waters closed over her, uniting her with her lost daughter.

***

The Brethren gathered in the central place as the turbocopter hovered overhead; this had never happened before. None of the Brethren were afraid – just curious. The turbocopter lowered to just the height of a man above the ground, dropped a huge package and sped off.

The Scientific Brethren were quickly on the scene with their decontamination apparatus, and, with their other equipment and instruments, ensured that the package was safe; only then was it taken away.

***

Soon there was official confirmation from the Scientific Brethren that the package had contained radon; radon for the radon engines! Far, far more Radon than had been lost in the storm. Perhaps with increased sensor prediction and another radon motor the life of the Sea Brethren could be extended longer than before the storm!

All the Brethren rejoiced at the news and marvelled at the strange visitation by the turbocopter. The Elders had decided not to tell the people of the message attached to the package; it had taken a while to decipher, even though it was a very simple one. It said, "Thank you."

A Funny Turn

"Mr Muckleton, would you mind if our students join us to discuss your case?"

"Not at all," said the patient, looking up from his hospital bed at the impressive entourage around him. "But please call me Clarence or even Clarie. Most of my friends call me that and none of them-"

"-Very well, Clarence and thank you," said the doctor. "May I introduce you to Professor Almond who is actually the senior doctor on this unit; unfortunately he was away on holiday when you were admitted, but will review your case with us today."

The professor looked up from reading the patient's records.

"You say that the patient has a mental blank – with total amnesia – lasting for 12 hours?" he asked, addressing the senior resident.

"Well, not quite," interrupted the patient, "it was more like 11 and three-quarter hours if you-"

"-Thanks," smiled the professor indulgently. "And you have admitted him for four days while doing all your tests?"

"Yes," said the senior resident, "and everything has turned out to be completely normal; his neurological examination was normal, and all blood tests and brain scans were totally normal." Confidently, he added, "We think this is a case of Transient Global Amnesia."

"Okay," said the professor, turning his back on the patient and ignoring him even more than was his usual custom, "tell me why you think it is a case of TGA."

"He presented on his own at A & E with the story that he had no recollection of events for the previous 12 hours. There was no history of head injury or other traumas, migraine, epilepsy or-"

"-Yes, yes," interrupted the professor, "and all your examinations were normal…"

"Yes, indeed, sir. Repeated neurological examination, all the blood tests, all the scans were totally normal."

"Well what, then, is missing that would clinch the diagnosis?"

The team looked at each other for help.

"An eye-witness account would have been helpful," opined one of the juniors.

"Yes, indeed – in fact critical!" stated the professor. "There is almost always some perseveration, some repetition of a statement or question; otherwise the patient's behaviour would seem entirely normal! Has he had no visitors whatsoever?"

"No sir, he seems to be a solitary sort of person who works as a senior clerk at Butters Accountancy. No-one has been to see him while he has been here."

A nurse came over and whispered in the senior resident's ear.

"Ahem. I take that back, sir; there is a lady waiting to see him outside."

"Then let's interview her, clinch the diagnosis, and clear this bed for someone else," decreed the professor decisively.

***

The professor, invigorated by his holiday and wanting to re-assert his expertise over his team, led the interview with time, patience and sensitivity. The "witness" was a very pretty young woman who apparently had worked with the patient. In fact, no-one had suspected that he had been ill and her eyes filled with tears when she learned that he had been in hospital without a single visitor. The picture emerged of a rather dull, timid and penny-pinching middle-aged bachelor who had few real friends and a reputation for being extremely boring. However, on the day in question, he had acted totally out of character, had made lots of friends, and persuaded them to help him "save the children."

"Did he repeat any phrases or activities?"

"Oh yes," said the young woman, her eyes brightening, "he kept saying over and over again that we must save the children."

"Okay," said the professor, turning to his entourage, "this confirms the diagnosis. Doctor Woodcock, please do the necessaries and discharge the patient."

***

Discharging the patient was easier said than done, as Clarence Muckleton had many, many questions. After 35 minutes of explanations, Doctor Woodcock was still there.

"And will it happen again?" asked the patient.

"Very, very unlikely indeed – in fact, less than one chance in 10 that it will recur," explained Doctor Woodcock for the third time.

"I still don't understand why it happened and what brought it on," said Clarence, driving the poor doctor to despair, as this too had been explained several times.

In a final act of desperation, the doctor resorted to a pen and paper and wrote down a list of possible precipitants, where he could find more information, and contact details should he need to re-consult.

Mr Muckleton went out of the hospital clutching his list with a thoughtful expression on his face; however, he had been given the "all-clear" and decided to go straight back to work.

***

As he walked through the office doors, an extraordinary thing happened: jaws dropped, people stood up, and then they began to applaud him. Clarence was mystified as they usually avoided eye-contact and ignored him.

Soon, a middle-aged lady with a kind face and a sumptuous figure, called Sylvia, came forward and said:

"Clarence, we all owe you such an apology; we never thought you had it in you. Word has got around and – so far – you have been promised at least £10,000 for Children in Need, a week on Saturday." She moved closer and whispered in his ear, "And I will fulfil my promise to you," furtively touching his buttocks.

***

From then on Clarence Muckleton became a real celebrity: everywhere he went, he was surrounded by smiles and offers of sponsorship money, but sponsorship for what? He did not dare to ask, and it was only through very circuitous routes that he finally discovered the truth: he had promised to do a skydive and parachute jump from 16,000 feet! This is the highest possible drop which could be made without oxygen and to the people who knew him, this seemed totally sensational! He could not believe that he had agreed to such an insane act as he was terrified of heights and had never even been in an aeroplane! What was he to do? How could he possibly get out of this situation?

Then he had an idea: maybe the neurologist would give him a medical excuse not to do the jump; after all, he had been the victim of a TGA. It was certainly worth a try. He hastily made an appointment to see the professor.

***

The professor, already alerted to the prolixity of his patient, was determined to keep the conversation as short as possible; conversations with patients like Muckleton could go on indefinitely, and the professor was a very busy man. Yet in spite of his experience, the professor was struggling to terminate the conversation amicably without yielding to the request for a medical "certificate" to avoid the jump.

Finally, in desperation, he took a big breath and said:

"I think, Mr. Muckleton, that there is a braver, more extraordinary Mr. Muckleton living inside your head which was brought on by this episode; all we have to do is to bring him back to life." Clarence opened his mouth to speak, but the professor would have none of it.

"There are well-known precipitants of this condition, and I am going to give you a list, and I want you to do all of them before the jump. The "other" Clarence Muckleton will then emerge, and you will enjoy your first ever skydive and parachute jump."

When you have nothing but straws to clutch at, even a single straw can be fantasized into a life-raft, and that is just what Clarence Muckleton did, clutching his list for dear life.

***

He made his preparations. He would do a three mile run on the day of the "dive" followed by a long, very cold shower; he would fast for 24 hours and then drink loads of coffee and some brandy. There was just one thing missing that was difficult to organise… apparently having sex was sometimes a precipitant of TGA…

"Sylvia, I am so sorry to bother you, but would you please come and visit me on the morning of my skydive to wish me luck."

"I would do anything to help a hero like you," came the reply.

***

And things did go according to plan, from the cheering of the crowd and the cries of "Good Luck, Clarie" to the "We love you Clarie" as he climbed into the plane.

Exhausted from his run, his fast, his cold shower, and his exertions with Sylvia, he seemed almost tranquil as the plane taxied and then took off.

The encounter with Sylvia had been amazing, and he was quite touched by the sweet words she had whispered to him.

Surely the returning hero would be able to repeat the encounter?

But what next? What if people began to expect this sort of thing from him? Maybe he should lose some weight and take up mountain climbing – or maybe even marathon running; perhaps pot-holing, a walk across a desert, or even a flight into space! He was feeling most peculiar, yet somehow so happy and optimistic that he "knew" that another attack of TGA had begun and that 'the other' Clarence Muckleton was taking over. At the very thought of this, he began to smile. "Where is all this going to end?" he mused.

The Inheritor

Silas Kent pulled on his cigarette and smiled contentedly into the blue smoke; times were good.

He sipped his coffee and surveyed his possessions from his panoramic top-storey orangery. As far as the eye could see, and indeed far beyond that, he owned the land – a most magnificent farm indeed with two thousand head of cattle, fifty employees, and more wealth than a hundred normal folk. He had good cause for contentment.

There had been no need of "book-learnin'" to achieve his massive estate, just simple hard work and application. He hired – and paid for – the very best, whatever the job, so as to ensure that it was done precisely to his specifications.

He made his way over to the elevator and barked an order in its direction. The doors flew open immediately. It amused him that the elevator was set to respond to his voice only; the servants and even Donoghue – his right-hand man – were forced to use the stairs!

The huge four-wheel drive was already prepared for him:

"Will you be taking Centaur with you, Mr Kent?" Kent nodded without looking up and shortly afterwards a huge Rhodesian Ridgeback jumped into the back of the truck, barking with joy to be going out with his master.

***

"Yes, it's just about getting things right," he mused as the tires squealed on the asphalt, "just about having things done properly."

He had no need of anyone else; his wife was away "shopping and sight-seeing" in Europe for a few weeks, his son was a lawyer in New York, and his daughter lived in Toronto with her husband and family.

He had been a tough father and ascribed his children's success to his rather austere management of their upbringing.

'You shouldn't be too close to your kids as it makes them soft' was his golden rule. And when it came to business he was even more impersonal: "When everything is working well, you don't need people," he deliberated. "You pay for the best, and you get things right." The question now was should he go into politics? He certainly had the money and allies in high places. It was true that he had attracted some opprobrium, though, as when he was asked about his occupation and he had answered, "Professional gas-guzzler." But people forget…

***

He parked, as usual, in a space for the disabled, feeling quite entitled to do so as he employed several (actually two) disabled workers on his ranch. He left the keys in the ignition and the car unlocked; no-one would dare steal from, or question, the behaviour of Silas B. Kent.

He was late, as usual, and skipped the apology, as usual, walking straight into the doctor's consultation room.

"Ah, Mr Kent," smiled the doctor with great professionalism hiding a foment of emotions playing behind his 'warm' welcome.

"Where's Jason today?" asked Kent in an irritated voice.

The older physician looked down at the floor for a few seconds.

"There was a family tragedy… you may have heard about it… unfortunately, he has to be away at the-"

"-Oh yeah, yeah, I seem to remember something about that…"

"I guess you have come for the results, Mr Kent?"

"You guess right, Mike. Just give me the all-clear then I can decide whether to run for government office."

A slightly startled look broke through the consummate professionalism of the very senior physician.

"Where shall we start, Mr Kent?"

"Start any place you goddam like, Mike; those tests cost me a fortune – X-Rays, breathing tests, blood tests, the whole damned shooting match. Now you just tell me they are okay and I'll get the hell out of this place!"

"Well, Mr Kent," said the doctor with all the qualified gravitas at his disposal, "if the tests were not normal, would you really want to know?"

"Want to know?, want to know?" he said with some stridency, "You bet I'd 'want to know' and I want you to fix them so they are damned well normal or get me to someone who can!"

The senior physician took a deep breath; this was not going to be easy.

"Okay, in brief, and roughly in order of importance, these are the results: you have a shadow on your lung which needs further investigations involving further X-Rays and probably a biopsy. Your blood tests are abnormal, and these do need further tests. Your breathing tests show that you do not have a great lung capacity and indeed that you have the lungs of a much older man, your abdominal aorta measures-"

Silas Kent interrupted, obviously angered by the news.

"Listen up. My father lived to be 92-years-old, and I live on the same farm he did and eat the same food he did. He was the fittest 90-year-old in the State… are you trying to tell me that I am somehow miraculously different from him?"

The professionalism dropped, and the physician became silent for a while and then spoke very slowly.

"I knew your father well… in many ways, he was the best friend I ever had. Even though he was 92, I did not want him to die, and I advised all kinds of interventions that caused him so much pain…" There was now a genuine moistening of his eyes. He continued, "I wouldn't want the same things to happen to you…"

"But I am only 67-years-old" Kent almost screeched, "And my father was 92. 92!"

"Yes," nodded that doctor, "but he never smoked, he worked on the farm and at every juncture he took my health advice which I gave from the heart... your situation is very, very different. Let's discuss things tomorrow or the day after when you have had a chance to think about matters. Yes, I'm sure that is the best thing to do."

Silas Kent glared at the doctor and stormed out of the consulting room.

***

"What the hell do I pay these guys for?" he muttered to himself, as his car screamed out of the town and nearly ran over a clump of pedestrians. He wondered if the older physician really knew his stuff... maybe he should return and see Jason, his usual physician. Yet there was something rather ominous in the words of the older man, something that struck him deeply. In fact, the drive home was perhaps the most unpleasant he could remember. Was that old guy telling him he was going to die?

He slammed the car door shut and barked out his order. "Get Nelson saddled up; I'll be down in 15 minutes."

"Yes Sir," chimed the hireling.

***

How on earth could he have health problems when he could spend hours in the saddle? How all his friends had been impressed when he told them he had been 'in the saddle' all day? And indeed he had, riding to the four corners of his mighty estate and drinking in the joy of ownership. However, he had forgotten that that had happened eight years earlier. He galloped in the direction of the hill country at quite a speed and very soon the horse was clearly tiring.

"So, can't keep up with me, Nelson old boy?" he mocked with a wry smile.

The terrain was becoming steeper, and the views were becoming even more spectacular. Kent dismounted; it was a mere 100 yards to the summit. He tethered the horse to a piton that had been spiked into the limestone and walked up the slope. By the time he reached the top, he was sweaty and breathless; indeed, he felt quite unwell in spite of his slow ascent.

He sat down, cupped his chin in his hands and looked down at the vistas below. Things were clearly not all right.

The idea of death was totally new to him as he always assumed he could buy his way out of any situation. He slugged on the whisky in his hip flask, felt a little better and tried to be philosophical. 'Sometime in the future, someone will be waking up in my bed, enjoying my home, my land, my possessions and it won't be me,' he reluctantly realised. To Silas Kent, this was a novel idea.

He took another slug from the hip flask. He looked out over the valley and in the distance saw his beautiful white home, topped by the glorious orangery, contrasting it with the lush green, irrigated swathe he had fashioned from the prairie. The bluebonnets, the prickly pear, the sage and the yucca all gazed back at him, all looking so 'right' under the azure-blue sky. Suddenly, the total beauty of it all hit him in the stomach like a runaway boulder and an exquisite tingling ran from behind his neck to down his spine: it was all so beautiful! For a while, he was almost in a trance, drinking in the spectacular beauty of it all, though something was still niggling at the back of his mind... oh yes, he was going to die – probably sooner rather than later.

And who would inherit his estate? His wife and children had no interest in his way of life... they would certainly sell it all off. Then some anonymous person or (God Forbid!) faceless organisation would take it over and his life's work would be lost forever.

His father must have felt similar emotions when he knew that he was dying, but at least he had continuity in his son – that surely helped him! But who was the inheritor before his father and who was before him?

It must have been some Redskins that 'owned' the land; indeed there was still an area known as "Indian Gulch" where there were allegedly Indian remains. Maybe generations of Indians had felt that same 'ownership' as he had enjoyed… who knows? Silas had previously had no interest in the history of his lands. Indeed, when asked for permission for archaeological work on his land, he had always dismissed them out of hand, but now…

**

"Emma, some guy from the University of Georgia wanted to do some archaeology on my place…"

"Yes, Mr Kent; he was from the Anthropology department at Georgia and he-"

"-Get him here tomorrow!" said Silas.

"Sir, that is a long way away; it will need a plane flight, he may have to cancel classes, he-"

"-Tomorrow," affirmed Kent without raising his voice.

**

"There is a Mr Cherokee Pete here to see you, Mr Kent."

"Thanks, Alice."

Silas B. Kent was a little hungover from yesterday's upheavals and now he even wondered if it had been a good idea to invite the "Anthropologist" to visit his lands. He took his time to dress; he was used to keeping people waiting.

By the time he arrived on the ground floor, Alice was clearly enjoying the company of the redskin and the sound of her tinkling laugh greeted him as the doors of the elevator sprung open.

The man stood up and surprised Kent by his very height; he was a good 4 to 5 inches taller than the landowner.

"I'm Silas Kent."

The big redskin reached out, took the rancher's hand into his own huge hand and shook it warmly.

"It is so nice of you to allow me to look at your property, Mr Kent," he said with seemingly genuine affection. Kent indicated with his head that the Indian should follow and they went outside into the warm sun.

Centaur bounded over and growled ominously at the stranger who walked towards the huge dog, whispering some strange words; in just a few seconds the Ridgeback was licking the Indian's hand with unexpected friendliness.

"You got a way with animals?" asked Silas.

"Yes," smiled the Indian matter-of-factly.

"George," barked Silas, "Saddle up Nelson and Fingal."

"Are you sure you want to ride on Fingal, Mr Kent, he has-"

"-Fingal is for this Indian," he gestured at his companion, "he has a way with animals."

***

"So, Mr Indian, what do I call you?"

"Call me Pete," said the Indian evenly, "I am not really a Cherokee."

"Okay, Pete, lead the way and tell me who you are and what you want."

'Pete' led the way at a gentle pace, up to the hill country; he wanted to have a general look at the landscape before they went to Indian Gulch. He talked about his background, his part Huichol Indian ancestry and of his studies at the University. He believed that there had been a settlement of the Huichol around here – further north than had ever been believed before. He wanted to explore the Indian remains at Indian Gulch and see what the truth was.

Silas Kent was not a good listener, normally, but this Indian held his attention and time passed very quickly. The Indian continually looked at his listener, noting and reacting to any change of expression, any subtle change of breathing or body posture; he showed his new friend the flowers and revealed their names and habits, taking a few samples of some cacti 'for his studies'. He showed him the trails of some animals, but made his whole dissertation fascinating to the older man.

"Best view is up top of this ridge," Silas announced dismounting.

They tethered their horses and began the ascent. The Indian was moving more quickly and soon the older man was sweating and in some discomfort.

"You okay?" asked the Indian with concern.

"I have an ankle sprain," said Kent, unapologetically trying to cover for his lack of fitness.

"I can't have you suffering on my account," said the Indian, and he scooped Silas into his arms, carrying him effortlessly to the top of the ridge.

The two men surveyed the area from the summit, with Silas pointing out the major landmarks, though the Indian seemed to already know most of them.

"I guess you are still hurting," said the Indian, handing over some small leaves he had picked. "Chew these… they are a little bitter at first, but you will soon feel the benefit!"

The Indian continued speaking, but Silas Kent increasingly felt distant; the words seemed to get through, but in a different way. As Pete spoke about the flowers, the glorious bluebonnets, and gaillardia and black-eyed Susan swaying in the sun, somehow the older man's eyes were opened to a different view of his land. He felt himself strangely drawn to this magnificent Indian who seemed to know so much.

"Can we go and see what you call Indian Gulch now? I don't want to tire you?"

"Yep, that's fine," said Kent.

***

Kent felt so much stronger and better as they approached Indian Gulch and was intrigued by Pete's description of the ancient Huichol culture and how important were their "dreams."

"Do you ever have dreams that come back and haunt you, Silas?"

Silas Kent found it quite difficult to speak, but anxious to please his 'guide', he dredged up some memories from the past.

"...yes, Pete, I do: I dreamed a few times about roaming around my land, free and nearly flying, almost like a wild animal."

"Not a blue deer?" asked Pete in amazement.

"Yes... yes I think it was like a blue deer," he struggled, trying to remember through a thick fog.

"And when you were flying, was it like being an eagle?"

Kent tried to think. "Yes... like a bright eagle flying high... where no one had ever been... and nothing mattered and time stood still." He paused at the strangeness of what he had said.

Pete looked stunned and stared deep into this eyes, then joined his hands as if in prayer.

"I believe that you may be the luminous eagle of the ancients," he finally said, lowering his forehead to touch the old farmer's boots. Such a 'truth' would help everyone. Pete finally looked up and added, "I believe this is the sacred place of the sacred ceremony: can you see how this semicircle of stones would have been the altar, and everyone would have been around it."

Pete quickly made a fire and warmed some beans. "Chew some more cactus medicine for the pain, Luminous Eagle,"

75

he suggested with some concern. Silas again noticed the initial bitterness and the feeling of improved health that followed. Was he being cured by this Indian?

"If your legs want to dance, then just let them," said the Indian smiling. For the first time in many years, Silas Kent found his legs actually wanting to dance; he kicked off his boots and began to move and sing – a totally meaningless song whose utterance surprised him. Time stood still.

Finally, he sat down, exhausted, and slipped into a light dreamy sleep.

"You have sung an ancient song of the Huichol, Luminous Eagle. You have indeed been sent from the old gods." But Silas was elsewhere, stalking the heavens and ghosting across far plains, lost in time and space with no ties, no roots, no life, no death; this was the immortal dance of the Huichol. He rode through time and suffered all the pain and joy of the ancient peoples and knew that he had become one of them, born of their soil. He swore he would help them.

***

The moon was high in the heavens as he rode his horse home; several of his servants were waiting for him. The Indian had gone but would return in two days to continue his research.

"We were worried about you," said Donoghue with some concern.

"Never worry about me," said Kent. "I feel better than I have felt in 50 years!"

***

"Okay," said the neurologist, happily, "you pass all my tests!" It had been a gruelling 90 minutes of history, questions, and examination of every aspect of neurological function.

"Okay," said Kent, "Am I fit and capable mentally?"

"Absolutely," affirmed the neurologist, "and I have produced a document to that effect as you requested."

"Thank you," said Kent, walking out with the paperwork.

***

"Have you discussed the changes to the will with your wife?" asked the lawyer with some alarm.

"Nope," replied Silas, "and neither shall you. This will be between you and me, except in the event of my death… are you clear about that?" he asked insistently.

"Yes, indeed Mr Kent, absolutely clear. You are an extremely valued client of ours, and so I rushed through your requests just as you wished."

"And you will keep a copy of my neurologist's report with the will?"

"Absolutely," said the lawyer, "It will remain in our most secure safe until you request it again."

Silas Kent smiled and walked out. The deed was done.

***

Muriel Kent had shortened her stay in Europe when she had heard about the strange behaviour of her husband, and indeed on her arrival she had informed her children of the bizarre turn of events. For the last few weeks, her husband had been living in Indian Gulch, the ancient site having been restored at some considerable expense.

"What do you make of Silas?" she asked. Her son had made the suggestion that their family friend, Mike Taylor MD and clinical neurologist, should visit Silas and assess his state of health – both mental and physical.

"Do you think he has gone mad?"

Mike Taylor sat down wearily; it had been a long day. Certainly, the Silas Kent he had just encountered was nothing like the old Silas Kent he had known for many years.

"Sometimes, we have to ignore the usual medical protocols to get to the bottom of exceptional circumstances, and I hope you appreciate that my views are completely 'off the record' as I-"

"-Yes, of course," said the son testily. "Just tell us what you can of the medical realities."

The neurologist took a deep breath.

"I gained access to his medical records and in the strictest confidence can tell you that Silas very likely has lung cancer and has refused further tests and treatment."

Mrs. Kent looked down at the floor and shook her head.

"I can also tell you that this is no longer the Silas Kent we all know and... and... love... this is a different human being."

"We are worried that he could make bad decisions about the farm in his current state of mind," said the son, his real concerns not having been addressed.

"Lung cancer is notorious for its propensity to spread to the brain, and I believe that the only way to account for Silas's behaviour is that this has indeed happened. He seems almost euphoric at the moment – totally peaceful and unconcerned about his usual preoccupations. I don't believe that he would make any rash decisions as I found him today. However, if he did, for instance, alter his will in a strange way, then I believe that such an alteration would be invalid in law due to his... 'diseased' state of mind."

There was a sigh of relief.

"I also believe that he does not have very long to live," he added solemnly. "Without treatment, he may have just a few months."

The relief in the room was almost palpable, and Muriel went over to the cabinet to get the good doctor a drink; she was already wondering what she would wear at the funeral and how she would spend the next chapter of her life. From what had been said, her husband surely did not have long to live.

But the thoughts of the Luminous Eagle were far from death as the chants and the dance beats echoed across the gulch. In the fire and the shadows, and fully charged with the cactus medicine, the world had become a very different and absorbing place.

Dream and reality met in a gentle embrace across the historic sky as the two Indians re-lived the history of their peoples and shared their dreams of reviving their culture and their fortunes. Luminous Eagle felt younger than ever; he had somehow forgotten to smoke his tobacco and his dancing and chores in the open air had improved his health. To him it was the healing of the cactus medicine which had wrought the profound changes in his health; but whatever the reason, he was reborn and empowered, and his new life was just beginning...

The Door

Anthony Idris Templeton-Lyle looked at himself in the mirror and smiled with satisfaction at his reflection. As captain of the high school basketball team, he was the perfect height and his shoulder-length hair and athletic physique made him the perfect 60s male. Moreover, his doting parents had ensured that his would be the most expensive tuxedo at the prom. His school grades had all been As (of course) and he was pre-destined to go to Yale or Harvard to study Law and inherit the family business. On the face of it everything was perfect, and indeed it was, almost.

Needless to say, he could have taken any girl to the prom – no girl in the county would have turned him down for sure. But he had delayed and delayed so that when it came to make a choice, all the hottest girls had been spoken for and he was stuck with the remainders – the subs bench if you will!

After much agonising, he had settled on Christina Moran. 'Stuck with' was perhaps a little unkind as Christina was not unattractive and indeed was a very accomplished ice-skater with a stunning figure; however, she was from a poorer family and was not in the 'Ivy League' class. Rumour had it that she was still a virgin! 'If that were the case,' thought Anthony, 'such a situation would certainly be remedied in the course of the evening!'

"Darling, hurry – you will be late!" called his mother from downstairs.

Of course he would be late; everything waited for Anthony.

He made one final check in the mirror, ensured that his wallet was replete with condoms and sauntered downstairs.

"Anthony," said his mother pronouncing the "th" as in "think" – "Anthony, you look a dream-boat… I just know that you will be the most handsome boy at the prom." He had long-since suppressed the irritation occasioned by his mother's pronunciation of his name in exchange for the richer rewards of her unfettered devotion to her only child.

"Go in and see your father."

Anthony went quietly into the television room; his father, as usual, was watching T.V. in the hope of better news from the war in Vietnam.

"See you later, Dad. Don't wait up for me," he offered.

"Okay, son," replied his father. "Don't do anything I wouldn't do!"

Anthony smiled at the bad old joke.

"How is your war going?"

"Ugh" grunted his father, "Not well at all; they need some of our supermen like you to go and sort them all out …. We really should stop pussyfooting around with those bastard Viet Cong," he added.

***

No-one could believe that she was going to the prom with the 'catch-of-the-year.' Christina had eyed him longingly for at least 18 months (though it seemed like much more) and believed that she was truly "in love" with him. 'Why had he asked her?' she had wondered many times since; maybe he had seen her ice-skating, though she'd never noticed him in the audience. Maybe he preferred a more innocent girl who would save herself for a special man? For whatever reason, tonight – prom night – was going to be the best night of her life.

"Is my make-up O.K.?" she asked.

"No, you should take at least half of it off!" said her mother, not really expecting to be obeyed.

"You look like a Fairy Princess," said her little sister, looking up wide-eyed at the beauty before her.

... and Christina really did look like a Fairy Princess; she had practiced putting on her make-up for weeks and tonight the effect was stunning. For this night, more than any other, she wanted everything to be perfect and she was becoming nervous when her date was clearly going to arrive quite late.

Then they all heard the growl of the sports car as it pulled up outside; Christina scampered up the stairs for a last check. There was an appropriate delay followed by a confident knock at the door. As the door opened, Christina could see him from her hiding place at the top of the stairs, his outline framed in the door by the setting sun behind him, an image that burned itself into her soul for years to come... an image that made her feel that her heart was ready to burst.

***

"You must be Anthony," said her mother, holding out her hand. "Christina has told me so much about you." Anthony smiled his well-practised heart-winning smile for older people.

"It is a pleasure to meet you Mrs Moran," he said deferentially.

"Christina won't be a moment. I think she is just putting on the finishing touches." She leaned forward and added in a whisper, "She has been so looking forward to this evening."

"Me too," smiled Anthony, disguising his true feelings with practiced deception.

"What a wonderful home you have here..." he added, "...so full of character." (How else could he compliment clutter, mess, and smallness?)

"Oh, thank you," said Mrs Moran. "What a charming boy you are!" Mrs Moran, like everyone else, was quietly falling in love with the young man and wondering what it would be like to go on a date with such a perfect example of American manhood!

Anthony made the most of the short wait to indulge his skills in small-talk with a social inferior before Christina appeared at the top of the stairs.

"Wow," he said looking up at her, "you look like you walked off a movie-set." And Christina really did look like a movie star, compelling Anthony to notice the stirrings inside his trousers and confirm that sex with this beautiful innocent would be the high point of the evening. But first, there was work to be done.

"Shall we?" he said offering Christina his arm.

The beautiful couple stepped smiling out of the door.

***

As they drove to the prom, Anthony asked all the right questions, enquiring about Christina's grades, her ambitions, what sort of music she liked, interspersed with compliments such as how beautiful she looked and how thrilled he was that she had let him take her to the prom; all well-practised, target-driven conversation.

They finally pulled up at the car park. "I hope you won't think less of me," he said quietly, as if revealing a dark secret, "but I am not as confident as people think I am, and if you will forgive me, I will cope better after a little shot of this." He took a hip-flask from his pocket.

"Of course, I forgive you; I am rather shy myself!" she replied with some vehemence. The drink was vodka, 'borrowed' from his father's extensive supply and was intended for Christina rather than himself. As they shared their guilty, intimate drink to 'boost their confidence,' Anthony made sure that Christina had a larger share; he planned to have her in the mood for a "fun" evening.

***

Everyone at the prom was on the lookout for Anthony, though those who knew him well would have predicted a late arrival. Finally, as he walked through the door and down the stairs formally linking arms with Christina, there was an appropriate ripple of interest. The couple wandered over to the bar and Anthony ordered two orange juices which would go well with the vodka; alcohol was forbidden, of course, but many students managed to sneak in some illicit booze and keep it from the watchful eyes of the chaperones.

They took their drinks and walked up to the balcony to watch the dancing. By now, a few of the students were already a little intoxicated and dancing with gusto and abandonment.

"Can you dance?" asked Anthony, torn between the possibility of showing off his own wonderful moves, and being let down by an inferior partner.

"Yes," replied Christina quickly guiding him down to the dancefloor, her inhibitions numbed by her first ever drink of vodka. And she could dance! Her athleticism, rhythm and grace from her ice-skating and her home practice in anticipation of this very moment made the couple look sensational; everyone stared as they went through their moves. Christina was a very intuitive dancer and more than equalled Anthony's prowess. The other students were astonished by the performance and some even wondered whether they had rehearsed together. It was quite clear now why Anthony had decided to bring Christina!

Anthony was thrilled at having such a stunning partner and being the focus of attention, though less so at being somewhat upstaged by his date.

He was sweating more than she as they went back to their seats.

Inevitably people kept coming up to Anthony and talking, but Anthony kept his attention on Christina and politely dismissed them.

"You have a wonderful sense of rhythm," said Anthony. "Do you play a musical instrument?" (He actually wanted to tell her about his own guitar playing.)

"Yes, I've played the piano for many years; I would love to play for you… I have heard you play guitar and sing – you are awesome!"

"Let's have another dance," he finally said. "You really are the belle of the ball!"

After a few more dances and drinks, he was finding her increasingly irresistible; he could smell her perfume and the alcohol had brought an inviting look to her eyes. Moreover, the stirrings inside his trousers were becoming quite pressing and hard to ignore.

"These people are getting on my nerves; shall we go somewhere quieter?"

"Oh yes – please!" answered Christina, intoxicated by the alcohol, the atmosphere, and the dance but above all with Anthony himself.

***

The couple sped off in the open-top sports car.

"Anywhere special you would like to go?" asked Anthony, although he had already decided.

"No," she answered, just thrilled to be alone with the boy she had been in love with for so long. A boy who had even exceeded her expectations and given her the perfect evening so far.

"Okay," he said, "let's go down by the lake and look at the stars."

Her heart was bursting with things she wanted to say, but she was afraid to spoil the perfect evening.

They came to a stop facing the lake, close to an old log cabin; it truly was a beautiful evening with a clear starry sky and a full moon shining on the water.

They got out of the car and walked hand in hand. He finally stopped and drew her close to him.

"You were the most beautiful girl at the prom and you were by far the best dancer... I never realised just how close I could feel to someone in just a few hours." He pulled her close to him and kissed her full on the lips; her reciprocation was total.

She shivered.

"You must be cold," said Anthony, "so thoughtless of me."

They walked towards the cabin; he took some keys from his pocket and opened the door.

"This used to belong to my grandfather and is a bit run-down," he apologised. Yet to Christina the door opened to a most wonderful place where they could be alone together. He switched on the light, stepped over to the fireplace, and put a light to the well-prepared fire.

"You will soon be warm," he said, putting some cushions on the floor in front of the fire.

Soon they were holding each other and staring into the flames.

Anthony looked into Christina's eyes.

"You know that there is nowhere I would rather be, and no-one I would rather be with, than here with you," he said holding her close.

"Me too," she enjoined.

The kisses became hotter as his arms ran down her back and he encountered her glorious firm buttocks; his trousers were bursting, but control at this stage would make for even more amazing sex. He exposed her breasts with no resistance and felt the beautiful innocent nipples as she began to breathe more rapidly.

"You are all woman – so perfect in every way," he breathed admiringly and began running his hand up the inside of her leg. At first, there was some resistance, but resistance to Anthony's charms would be futile.

His expert fingers were soon giving an at-first reluctant pleasure to her womanhood.

"Now I know you really like me," he purred into her ear, acknowledging the moistness of a woman aroused. There was no time for a condom; this was the magic moment as he entered her to a suppressed squeal of pain. He remained motionless inside her.

"I would stay here forever if it were possible," he whispered. She smiled in the darkness and held him even tighter. "Any man would go to hell and back for a woman like you."

***

Those three hours were the quickest and most exquisite of Christina's life; the beautiful things Anthony said to her and the feelings of being close to someone you love. She felt so wonderful about saving herself for her one true love. In the throes of wonderful sex, he had responded to her question that 'he could barely wait until tomorrow' to see her again.

Anthony complimented himself on his romantic language; anyhow, he had nothing better to do.

***

They had several 'dates' in the cabin by the lake and truly even Anthony marvelled at the quality of the sex. However, he really did not want to be seen in public with Christina and after the fourth date (and under an umbrella of excuses) did not see her for several weeks.

***

Anthony had not worried about the draft. He assumed that his father would somehow find a loophole if he were selected to serve his country in Vietnam. When the draft papers did arrive, however, the conversation with his father had been a disaster; the old man felt that he – Anthony – should be proud to serve his country and would have no part in 'draft-dodging.'

As always Anthony had remained outwardly cool and his father had congratulated himself on persuading Anthony of the noble task of service he was about to embark upon.

But Anthony had other plans.

***

'One last time,' Anthony had thought, before he put his plans into action; Christina would always cancel what she was doing for Anthony even at short notice. He held her wonderful naked body for what he assumed would be the last time. She seemed different.

"Is something bothering you?" he asked, feigning interest.

"Yes, Anthony," she said, holding him closer, "I think I am pregnant." She paused. "And I just don't know what to do…"

Anthony was silent for a while, wondering how much money he would get from selling his sports car.

"We will think of something," he said with a quiet confidence, "I would not let you down."

She held him tighter and kissed him hard on the lips.

***

As always, self-preservation was Anthony's primary objective: he would not put his life in danger in a far-off war; he would not be shackled to parenthood at the age of 18; he would not – any longer – be accountable to his adoring, but stifling, parents. His alibi was soon arranged; he would tell his parents that he was going on a fishing trip with his friend Jack, but would actually sell his sports car and get a motorbike in part exchange. The money from the deal would get him safely to Canada where he would start a new life. The only people who didn't adore Anthony were the folks who hadn't met him yet. Canada would be the answer.

"Don't worry, Christina, I have never loved anyone as I love you. Something will work out."

They said their goodbyes for the last time.

The part-exchange went well. The surplus amount of cash certainly seemed adequate to launch his new life. There was no time for delay, however, and Anthony's escape would begin at once. He would head up to the west coast of Canada and meet up with kindred spirits… a future full of unknowns, excitement and above all freedom.

As he sped along the highways with the wind blowing through his hair, Anthony felt the total freedom for which he had always longed: freedom from school, from expectations, from studies but above all freedom from his parents and the boring society in which they festered. Indeed as he experienced hunger, thirst, cold and real discomfort for the first time in his life, it was the hatred of his parents which kept him going with never a look back. 'My father is a total moron' was his recurring mantra and as he smouldered from the 'Vietnam betrayal,' he resolved never to return.

***

Christina listened attentively to the silence of the telephone and of the doorbell; he was the love of her life and would stand by her – he had promised. Nothing could stop him returning.

Maybe they would run away together or maybe just get married; she only knew one thing for certain - that she wanted him more than ever and needed him in her arms.

***

The winters were mild on the West Coast and the damp temperate climate made living quite bearable and easy, especially on the island where Anthony found himself. There was cheap weed aplenty, and for the first few months with his kindred spirits, his freedom of body was well-matched with his freedom of soul as his drug-charged brain scarcely touched base with reality.

What discussions they had and how they could make the world a better place – peace, love, freedom and their own generation of music that told the politicians what they should do.

***

"May I come in?" asked Mrs Moran of the expensively dressed lady who answered the door.

"Are you collecting for some charity?" replied Mrs Templeton-Lyle, stepping aside to let the stranger in.

"No, not at all," was the reply. "It is about Anthony."

The senior lady started.

"Do you know where he is?" Mrs Moran asked trembling.

"No, I have no idea," came the reply.

The two ladies shared their separate griefs; they allowed themselves a Martini each and then shared some more of their feelings. Even though there was nothing to be done, they both felt better for saying what had been close to their hearts.

***

Living in such a commune, it seemed churlish to even think about the future; there was weed and food and full intellectual exploration of all the subjects he had been denied. How dull his old classmates seemed! But there was a time when his money was beginning to give out and there were increasing pressures for him to earn some money in the Big City of Vancouver.

"You'll get there in a couple of hours on your bike and with your charm, you'll get enough in tips in a week to last us a year!"

Anthony felt slightly rejected as he made his way to the city, clutching the hostel address and the memory of his ability to charm anyone and hopefully turn his charm into money.

"I always knew my son was no coward. Now we can tell the world that he left so he could get away from that tramp Christina!" Anthony's father was jubilant. Now, he understood.

He held his wife in an embrace of shared sorrow.

"He will come back to us someday – he really will!" he added.

Of course, they would help financially with the child: if it were a boy they would call it Anthony and if a girl then it would be Antonia. Then all would be made public that his son was no draft dodger.

***

Anthony was amazed how difficult it was for him to get any kind of employment; he had been so used to people knowing who he was, and how doors would always fly open for him, that what he was now experiencing was rather new and unpleasant. Indeed, he really had to take a hard look at himself and how an unfriendly outside world might perceive him. In desperation, he had his hair trimmed and his newly-acquired straggly beard shaved off. Even then, he was only employed in the kitchens in a most humble capacity, but he knew that once the employers got to know him, they would employ – and reward him – appropriately.

***

"And that hussy of a daughter of mine never shed one tear of shame for what she has done to the family," her mother had confided to her parish priest.

But Christina, once she realised that she had been betrayed by her true love, felt a far greater pain than could possibly express itself in tears; this kind of loss was far worse than having someone die – even someone you really cared about. Tears could never do justice to this level of pain.

***

Eventually, an opportunity did present itself to Anthony, to work as a waiter in the restaurant. By now he was fairly desperate to make more money and achieve some 'recognition' which he had always taken as his God-given right but which now he realised he must fight for.

So he deployed his natural charm and instinctive ability to make people feel special and was quickly – if unofficially – the head waiter's right-hand man. Admittedly it was only as a waiter, but his star was beginning to rise again.

***

And so it happened that Christina gave birth to a perfect baby girl called "Antonia." Once she had realised that having the baby was the only choice, she became a very good parent, did all the right things, and soon became a very competent and devoted mother. There was plenty of support from Anthony's family who helped both financially and in the day-to-day care of Antonia; they had lost their only son and a grand-daughter became a real outlet for their grief.

***

"We have Spencer Twentyman coming tonight, Anthony. And in case you didn't know, he is the most important newspaper proprietor on the West Coast… I expect you to take good care of him." The head waiter looked Anthony in the eye to make sure he had understood, but Anthony always understood situations like that.

In fact, it was very easy to make a fuss of such a man – intelligent, well-informed, and very curious about Anthony himself. He quickly found out that Anthony was from the mid-West – even though Anthony had mollified his accent to sound more like a Canadian. Not only that, but he had spotted that he was a draft dodger. Over the forthcoming weeks, Twentyman visited the restaurant numerous times and the conversations – interrupted by the meals of course – led very naturally to Anthony being invited to have a coffee with the great man the following day. An invitation that was readily accepted.

***

It had been more than three years and no-one had heard from Anthony. The initial reaction of the community was of total shock at the disappearance of their brightest and best; nothing like this had ever happened before. Then came the speculations and rumours from every quarter and even after three years of silence, the interest did not wane.

"He might as well be dead even if he isn't!" his father had declared to Mrs Moran. She, in turn, had confided to her family that "Anthony's father thinks he is dead."

Then there were rumours and speculations about how he might have died and one theory that seemed to stem from nowhere was that he was killed in a brawl in a foreign country when someone insulted America.

When it finally came back to his father that his son 'had died fighting for America,' he took the story to heart and repeated it to his drinking friends with some embellishment.

***

The coffee had gone very pleasantly, followed by liqueurs, and the newspaper magnate was not only smart but could recognise talent.

"It's clear that there is more to you than just waiting tables," Spencer said to Anthony. "I wouldn't be where I am now if someone hadn't given me a break and I'd like to do the same for you. I want you to put together a column for my newspaper. Just once a week and you can carry on with your old job. I want to give my readers real insight into what is happening in Washington DC, your capital city."

"I have closed the door on that part of my life," said Anthony, "I have no interest in returning to America – ever. I have changed my name and I feel like a true Canadian."

Spencer noted that the words were spoken mechanically, and probably had been said many times before.

However, Spencer explained that he already had some staff members in Washington and it would merely require that Anthony correlate all the news and gossip and turn it into a readable section for the newspaper.

Anthony realised that this opportunity might not arise again; allies like Twentyman don't come along too often. So he set to work.

***

The advantage of being taken out of social circulation is that there are no social distractions, and Christina now threw all her spare time and energy into ice-skating. Her coach soon recognised her potential and there was talk of her gaining a top scholarship and even training with the national team. Christina just wanted to put the past behind her; to be so vilified even by her own family was hurtful and she knew that deep down she was a good person who would always commit at the deepest levels to what was important to herself and her loved ones.

When she heard that Anthony had been killed defending America, she drove her little car to the cabin by the lake and looked across the moonlit water. She even found the cabin where they had spent so many wonderful hours and pushed open the door. She stood for a while and looked into the darkness, paralysed by the beautiful memories that came flooding back. Finally she stepped outside, but was quite unable to bring herself to close the cabin door. She walked slowly backwards to her car, her gaze fixed on the room and feeling that part of her would be forever trapped inside it.

***

'A full time journalist - And a good one!' figured Anthony. It had come as no surprise that Spencer was gay and that Anthony's financial 're-positioning' might have been related – at least in some small part – to his acquiescence to the boss's sexual demands. Anthony always prided himself on his flexible behaviour and in the greater scheme of things these 'concessions' were a small price to pay for the considerable financial rewards of promotion – Big Time promotion with an excellent salary!

***

Christina smiled at herself in the way she revelled in, and responded to, the applause of the crowd; it somehow validated who she truly was and people were soon willing to gloss over her previous mistakes and see her as the skating celebrity she had become. Once, for an encore, she skated with her skating-prodigy daughter, the seven-year-old Antonia and the photos were splashed all over the press. Even without that, she would have made the Olympic Team; she was not only dedicated, a true professional, but also an inspiration to all the others.

***

Anthony was effectively running the newspaper and learning the tricks of the trade all the time; his man-management skills were innate and of the highest order, but he learned very quickly what made newspapers sell and how to get to the guts of a good story. He was now living with the boss, but sacrifices had to be made and the work was incredibly rewarding. The boss himself realised that Anthony was a gift from heaven for the newspaper and became increasingly remote from day-to-day management.

***

Even if Christina had not won a medal, her value to the team was enormous as she took the pressure off everyone else – she was the one the press wanted to interview and photograph. Indeed, had it not been for an unfortunate slip, she might well have gained a gold medal rather than her bronze, but the newspapers loved the story anyway and her fame only increased.

***

Anthony surveyed his team: they were all top men, good copy-writers, influential individuals trusted by their whole readership and the many newsworthy people who wanted 'to have their side of the story told.'

'Yet,' he thought, 'do any of them really know me or like me?' Sure their jobs depended upon the young American, but outside of that, did any of his new 'friends' care about him at all? Even the boss had moved on and now spent most of his time in Mauritius with his new boyfriend, and although not actually gay himself, Anthony felt a sharp pain of rejection and a pang, almost of longing, for his real home where once he had been truly loved.

He pondered what had happened to his last 12 years and as he looked in the mirror, he couldn't help but notice his stained teeth from coffee and coke and neglect, nor the sallow, lined complexion from his inability to curtail his cigarettes. His hair loss and weight gain were also clear; he had aged quite spectacularly. Yes, he could understand why the boss had moved on to someone younger and more handsome. Still he had retained the glory of his intelligent sensitive eyes he thought to himself.

***

"What about Christina Moran?" asked one of his sub-editors. "That would make a great cover story!"

Anthony had been trying to blot that whole thing out, even when she had appeared on the front of Time Magazine under the banner headline: "The Darling of America" and been given the most adulatory of interviews.

Anthony thought for a while as everyone looked to him for a decision.

"Good idea," he finally said. "Get me an interview with her and I'll go down and see her... though I love you all dearly I could do with a break." He smiled and they all joined in politely.

She was already three minutes late for the interview he noted with some slight irritation and some unexpected disquiet. He always arrived on time – it was simply to do with professionalism – and he was always interested in the timekeeping behaviour of others as it gave him some insight into how they felt about the forthcoming interview.

The flight and all the arrangements had gone like clockwork – as he had expected – so his anxiety level surprised him. She would not recognise him – indeed he scarcely recognised himself with his new beard and the facial changes of stress and neglect – and the interview would run smoothly with some good copy for his newspaper. That was the plan anyway.

She finally breezed into their private room 25 minutes late, yet with a smile and a single word: "Kids!" that wiped the slate clean, and further apology was rendered superfluous.

The usual courtesies were exchanged with particular warmth and the skills of two people totally adept at the interview format. And, of course, Christina was quite happy for the meeting to be recorded.

Anthony – now "Gareth" since his change of name – had read his research briefs meticulously and the conversation flowed effortlessly. She had answered all the usual questions so many times before it was easy for both of them… but where was the story? Could he open some emotional portal inside her to achieve his "scoop"?

"How old is your little girl now?" he asked.

"Antonia is almost 12-years-old and she is wonderful; not that my twin boys are any less, but she is such a beautiful skater and a wonderful person..." Christina's eyes became soft and her voice dropped. "She is like a superior person of me, or rather the kind of person I could have become if things hadn't happened the way they did." She looked down at the floor in some sadness.

"And would you say that this is a happy ending?" Gareth asked innocently.

Again her voice lowered and her eyes softened further.

"Oh yes indeed." She nodded her head slowly a few times with a wry smile. "I have this incredible family. My career has exceeded my wildest dreams and I have found love beyond what I thought would be possible," she added.

Gareth felt a slight lump in his throat and felt a little more nervous; for a few moments there was an awkward silence. As if to break it she said:

"By the way, I just love your Canadian accent; it always strikes me as so refined." She looked at him full in the eyes for the first time, "You have very beautiful eyes," she added, and after a pause, "in fact you remind me of someone and I just can't think who." She thought for a moment, then frowned.

"Of course, of course," she finally said, shaking her head in disbelief, "you remind me of one of the most wonderful and important men in my life."

She stopped for a moment, obviously overcome by powerful emotions. Anthony held his breath:

"Antonia's grandfather," she said very quietly,

Christina went on to explain that when his son Anthony had been killed defending America, Antonia's grandfather and his wife had become the perfect grandparents, helping not only financially, but emotionally, and explaining how the everyday activities brought the two families closer together. "They just couldn't have done more," she finally added. "I sometimes wonder if their love of Antonia may have somehow compensated for the loss of their son."

They both sat in silence for a while and Gareth seemed rather lost in his own thoughts. Christina decided that the interview was probably over and moved towards the door. She opened it and looked at the bloated, caricature of a journalist who looked so terribly sad. She waited a while and then walked through the door but could not bring herself to close it. She stepped back into the room and saw that there were tears streaming down the old man's face.

Could she leave him like this?

Yet she knew from her own experience that the most sacred tears, from the deepest wells of our sorrows, do not reach our eyes. 'He would cope,' she thought to herself; she stepped outside, whispered a final goodbye across the room and closed the door with a final click.

Journey to Callisto

She smiled to herself. "Alone at last," she thought. K44 was big enough to take five passengers – maybe eight at a stretch, but she was – mercifully – alone with everything she needed, everything for her serene inner world. Here, at last, there was no clutter, no contamination from the outside world; here she could be authentically her true self.

Of course the mission – to the Jovian moon of Callisto to deliver the raw materials for robot-making in Cyber City – was important; and even more important, she would be returning with a cargo of super-robots – the very latest designs – for evaluation on Earth! But such thoughts were far from her consciousness as she prepared for lift-off. With a name like "Vega" she would have inevitably ended up as an astronaut, but her true expertise – many had called it "genius" – was cybernetics. Nowadays, with such advanced computer controls of spacecraft, the training for even advanced astronautics was a mere three months; the only other requirement was to be physically fit, and Vega was outstandingly that! But to be an expert on robotics had a far higher status than a mere astronaut and boosted her profile for far higher remuneration.

As K44 quietly began its journey, Vega decided to do one last duty before she could enjoy the journey to the full.

"Mintaka Hedron speaking," intoned the voice.

"Vega here," she replied.

"My dear little sister," replied the voice with much feeling, "the brightest star in the sky."

Vega often felt uncomfortable speaking with her brother as he was by far the most effusive person she knew. She had surmised that this was due to his job as a CAD (Community Assignment Director), someone who was forced to deal a lot with emotional people.

"Where are you now?" he asked.

"Just setting off for Callisto. Do you need finances?"

"No, we are fine; just thanks so much for all your help in the past." Vega truly did not care whether she saw her brother and his family ever again, but there was an absurd family loyalty that kept her 'in touch' and 'supportive' – behaviours which she innately despised.

"Good," she said.

"Vega, please, please look after your fabulous self as our worlds would be so much poorer without you, we-"

"-Yes," she interrupted with exasperation, "I'd better go as I have things to do."

She rang off. Duty done.

***

A few minor checks later and then it was all "Vega-time"; she initiated her "surround screen" and switched to "My Garden." This had always been her favourite place; some regarded it as quirky and old-fashioned to love a garden so much, but this was her very special place. In fact, she had not visited her garden 'in reality' for the past two years, but her robots obeyed her every instruction to the letter, and the garden responded by becoming her own little paradise.

Now, she could wander through the beds of roses without a scratch, smell their amazing perfumes, and note how the robots had kept her garden totally free of weeds. Her beautiful lilies cascaded a stunning fragrance all around her – even more than in 'real' life – and she could 'walk' down the gently sloping lawn to the stream.

She frowned, but then began to smile as she remembered that all traces of "The Man" – everything that he had touched or defiled – had been expunged from her garden. When Love turns sour, when betrayal and clumsiness turn it to hatred, such memories have no part in your garden. Surgical excision of an unsightly mole was how she had described it to herself and smilingly had had him killed on a mission to Ganymede.

She had wondered about having him kill himself because of regrets at hurting her, but a speedy and clinical extirpation had been her final decision; the facts were unimportant – just her own "reality" which she could choose.

Now she could sit by the stream in total harmony. Bio-Tec advances had given her the option of a "time-crush" for the journey to Callisto, but Vega wanted to savour every microsecond and took the "time-dilation" option.

***

Yes, the blissful garden certainly put her in a wonderful state for the journey allowing her to catch up on some of the latest cybernetics research and other information she needed at her fingertips for the conferences in Cyber City.

She had finally had enough study, moved over to her "special" couch and flipped another switch:
"Pleasure me, Rigel," she said, "Protocol 7."

"Yes Commander," answered the manly voice and the perfected male of her fantasies appeared on the screen, smiling at her. She closed her eyes and felt his breath on her neck and his hands subserviently exploring her body; the "special couch" had been programmed perfectly, and the script from Rigel computed to surprise and delight her.

Relaxing after a wonderful orgasm, she reflected on how pointless so-called human relationships were, with all their sorry imperfections and nonsense; how superior was a "sanitised" date with her cybernetically-planned robot accomplice. Peace and tranquillity.

***

She did wonder whether Cyber City might have changed in her absence; after all, it had been six years since she had studied and taught there – a very happy year of her life she recalled. Intellectually, it had also been the most interesting time of her life as Callisto was the embarkation point for exploration of the solar system and beyond and therefore had been earmarked as the centre for robot research and development. She wondered what made her most happy these days and it was difficult to say; far easier to say what made her unhappy, like her liaison with Merak – "The Man" – which had ended in tears with feelings of revulsion and betrayal… she would never go down that pathway again.

***

"Welcome to Cyber City, Commander Vega," said the greetings official after an uneventful docking. The smile was totally empty and token; indeed, one of the joys of Callisto was the attenuation of those pathetic human emotions that so contaminated human existence.

She was taken to her cell chambers and noted the improvements that had taken place in her absence – everything planned, efficient and cross-checked. Even Rigel would be available should she need him.

She took a long, old-fashioned bath and dressed in the uniform that had been laid out for her.

'I'll check around the city before I take the sleep,' she decided.

***

The city had certainly changed, and with advanced robotics continually building and slavishly following orders, this was hardly surprising. The city had expanded both laterally and vertically and though she had seen pictures, this – the real thing – quite took her breath away; she could fully understand how all the young intellectuals felt that 'this was the place to be.'

She wandered into a 'bar' that had been a frequent haunt of hers previously and noted how much bigger that too had become with so many cubicles and gadgets to deliver any game, any experience, any sensation. Yet the big difference, and the one she was slow to realise, was there was no communication between any of the people there – none. Each person was there 'for their own thing.' In fact, it was crazy that these places were still called 'bars' – like in the old days when people would drink alcohol and talk and sing and argue. Long ago, the alcohol had been replaced by various "benzo-pops" – harmless mind-altering drugs which didn't destroy liver and brain and make people violent. Then the modern bar slowly evolved, where every conceivable pleasure, experience, and mind-alteration could happen at the flick of a switch.

"How many people come here?" she asked someone standing by one of the booths, but from the look on their face, she knew that she had been inappropriate and quickly apologised. It was not the same as before, and she felt that the place had maybe outgrown even her.

She went back to her cell chamber, switched on the computer and ordered:

"Sleep please; 5 hours!"

Soon she was asleep with only pleasant dreams.

***

The "lecture format" was still used for learning in Cyber City; it allowed researchers and other experts to present their arguments and have them subjected to the interrogation of their peers. Of course, the speakers were the very best and their presentations were totally engrossing. Then she saw him: Merak – "The Man" – and a wave of anger and revulsion ran through her body. How dare that creature intrude on her life with his miasma of crudity. How dare he still be alive!

"Hello," she said dispassionately as they walked out. He nodded. Neither smiled. "I thought I'd had you killed off, on a journey to Ganymede," she said flatly.

"You'll have to try again. I had you killed off on Titan, and now I scarcely recognise you."

'…human relationships are the pits,' she reflected sadly, noting that facts sometimes intruded on her personal "reality."

Though her stay on Callisto went very rapidly, she was quite happy when the time came to return to Earth; she almost looked forward to hearing from her brother again… "I'm becoming quite old fashioned," she mused.

Then the bombshell. Her orders were to share her journey back to earth with a student. There was no room for argument; the student was going to study cybernetic engineering for a year on Earth, and as there was 'plenty of room on K44.' She would accompany Vega on the journey. Vega was furious that her peace and calm would be disrupted but there was no choice.

"My name is Commander Vega," she said holding out her hand with no hint of a smile. "Please stay in your cabin whenever possible as I have much study to do."

"Of course," said the younger woman. "My name is Tessler, should you ever need it." She smiled a genuine smile which seemed rather pleasant to Vega.

***

They were three Earth days into the journey before they spoke.

"May I please request your help, Commander?" asked Tessler, "I am having some problems with some backup circuits in bio-robotics."

There was no escape, and Vega listened and explained how to approach these particular problems. Tessler was so attentive and quick to learn that the instruction was far from unpleasant and the two women clearly had a lot in common; in fact, Tessler reminded Vega very much of her younger self. As the conversation began to flow freely, Vega found herself – for the first time in many years – speaking quite fulsomely about some of the broader issues in cybernetics. The younger woman seemed to know a startling amount about Vega, and the look of – dare one say it – adulation, almost adoration, on her face made Vega feel better about herself than she had done for many years.

Each day, Tessler had her 'tutorial' and Vega began to look forward to them. Indeed, some of the discussions became quite broad and philosophical.

"What makes you happy, Commander Vega?" asked the younger woman.

Vega thought for a while and then explained that the peace and stillness of her garden, her inner serenity, and freedom from conflict were the most special moments to her.

"And what makes you happy, Tessler?" she finally asked.

Tessler thought for a few moments and then choked back some tears.

"Being with you, Commander Vega, is the happiest I have ever been. I have studied your life and admired your achievements, how you conduct yourself, and I would love to be more like you."

There was a silence as the two women moved very slowly towards each other and then embraced.

"I would dearly love to see your garden and share your tranquillity," she finally whispered in the commander's ear.

***

Then they did everything together, spending their meals, their quiet times, and their sleeping times together, each one hoping that they would never wake up from the dream and that the journey would last forever.

***

"Emergency! Emergency!" cried the robotic voice, "Space debris, damage considerable, preparing damage report."

The most dangerous part of space travel was re-entry into the Earth's lower exosphere and upper thermosphere. Considerable debris from defunct satellites could still destroy any spaceship and the two women were aware of the potential catastrophe which seemed to have struck their vessel. They listened calmly to the report; it was a risk every astronaut had to accept.

"Sector Six has been destroyed and disconnected. There is only life support for one person to return to Earth. The decision must be made and will become critical in seven minutes."

They looked at each other in horror.

"You must live on Commander Vega; your life is far more important than mine and I will take the extinction."

"No, Tessler. You are younger and with so much to give, it is for me to die so that you might live."

They sat in silence for a while, then the younger woman spoke.

"Emergency Code states that I must always sacrifice myself for a human when there is a choice. Commander Vega, I am the new Bio-Robotic which we have been developing on Callisto, and I am totally replaceable. Even my essential bio-vectors are taken from you, Vega, and therefore it is you who are unique and irreplaceable."

Vega was silenced, then said:

"I love you, Tessler, and I love you not for what you are but for whom you are... I will take the extinction."

Tessler held Vega in a grip of such strength that she knew it was the grip of a true Bio-Robot. There were tears streaming down the robot's face as she realised that she had passed the final test of Robotics - the willingness of a human to sacrifice its life for the robot. They held each, lost in Love's embrace as time stood still. Finally, Tessler broke the silence:

"There may be another way," she finally said, leading the Commander by the hand to the computer room.

"I think I can de-animate into the computer and suspend my functions until we arrive on Earth."

Vega watched in horror as the robot made the connections and began to de-animate; she had never heard of this protocol but desperately hoped it would work more than anything she had wanted in her entire life.

**

And that is how the pair came to survive the space-mishap and enter into legend as "The First," the new world of true cyber-love which would so often surpass the frailty of imperfect biological relationships. As the craft descended into its final approaches, they both knew that the world awaiting them would be very different from what they had known before; it was full of unknown challenges and excitements. Inevitably, it would mean a new era for themselves, for humanity, and for cybernetics.

The Stranger

(Story dedicated to the original Jackie)

I was born an alcoholic. Maybe it was some solar storm that ripped apart my foetal chromosomes and stapled them together in a clumsy fashion that caused it; maybe it was an astrological singularity with Arcturus and Mars in a rare conjunction that did it. Who knows? But, for whatever reason, I was born an alcoholic, though it took me 11 years to find out.

Then, the family party and the leftover drinks which only adults were allowed; the furtive gulps and… Nirvana! Immediately I felt like everyone else pretended to feel, except no cares, no worries … like a God celebrating his day of rest. There was nothing else I could ever want or hope for. This was the end of the line.

I hasten to add, that I am a very unusual alcoholic; pain, discipline, and self-control are easy for me. How else could I have skated so effortlessly through medical school? How else could I have become one of the best ophthalmologists of his generation? How else could I have become – dare I say it – a man so popular, with so many favours owed? I would never shirk a challenge, work, or a favour, so it was all so easy for me. Even my "fall from grace" and the removal of my medical license gave me no pain. Status never bothered me, and now I am just an "expert on the iris" and that may well be my final destination.

***

It was a routine call. Immigration had asked me to look at a "customer's" iris pattern which didn't fit with their computer model. I remember feeling quite bored as I went to the examination room, reflecting that I abstained from alcohol for three-and-a-half days of every week to fulfil my job commitments… what a waste of good drinking time. However, it was "important for national security" that everyone entering the country should have their iris identity check so that undesirables could be identified and excluded. All the same, this iris check was likely to be tedious.

But this was different. This was an iris the like of which I had never seen. In fact, it was not an iris as we know it; it was totally homogenous – no contraction furrows, no crypts, no pupillary frill. It was as a child might have drawn an iris with no knowledge of the true anatomy. Yet the pupil contracted normally to bright light, and there was no sign that this was an implant or that there had been any outside interference with this eye. To my understanding, it was impossible that any hostile government could have tampered with a human eye to produce such an effect. I was totally perplexed. Immigration just needed an answer: could I be sure this man was not a security risk?

***

Ophthalmology was an easy choice for me – a finite subject which I would learn to perfection; not only that but I have the ability to work in pictures, and whether interpreting the appearance of the retina or performing eye surgery, these aptitudes would stand me in good stead. All my bosses recognised my potential very quickly; some were even a little jealous, but they all gave me glowing references, as they were honest men at heart. My star rose rapidly as my reputation developed – both as a diagnostician and as a skilful surgeon. How the money flowed in; money I didn't want or need. People thought I was generous, but it is easy to give away things you don't value. My needs were so very, very simple.

***

The man smiled evenly at me.

"Where are you from?" I asked.

"It tells you all this on my passport," he answered untroubled.

"I would like to examine the back of your eye in more detail" I stated, scarcely even as a request.

"As you wish," he smiled.

Now I have looked at thousands of retinas in my career and never, ever failed to see them; yet here I was unable – completely unable – to see it. I put in some eye drops to dilate the pupil and paralyse the eye muscles. Still, I could see nothing of the retina!

"Mr Janek," I finally said with some exasperation, "I will need to do some further tests on you – a physical examination and some blood tests."

"Mr Schlebb," he said, chidingly, "as you are no doubt aware, you must show respect for the beliefs and creeds of others, and I do not give permission for any examination other than my eyes as stated by your immigration rules."

The man was totally charming, but I was becoming rather irritated, mainly because I was puzzled by the biological conundrum before me.

"What is your ethnic and religious background?" I queried.

"My answers would not help your curiosity, nor are they needed to fulfil your tasks, Mr Schlebb," he replied plainly.

He smiled the most beautiful disarming smile I had ever seen – or maybe I had before in some strange dream or memory – but the effect was most wonderful.

***

"Will you please buy me a drink?" she asked, "I will give you the money."

I smiled. "I will buy you a drink, but I will pay," as she was probably underage and angling for something alcoholic.

She gave a token 'thank you' and sipped her fruit juice in silence. She looked rather thin, and I worried she might even be anorexic.

"Are you hungry? Can I buy you dinner?"

She looked into my eyes for half a minute – a full thirty seconds!

"I do not want a pick-up, I am not a whore, and I may not want to speak to you. If that is clear, you may buy me dinner."

I laughed out loud at someone so fiercely outspoken; I had been much like that myself until medical school had forced its compromises upon me. I thought back to those early days and how quickly I had learned the best behaviours to stay out of trouble. In fact, my learned "people-skills" coupled with my other qualities had soon made be loads of "friends"; the quotation marks are only in place because people have to get on with their lives. They go through phases – partners, marriage, money, children – and I shared none of these travails, so all my "friends" eventually dropped away. There were so many "I owe you one's" given in their leavings – genuine promises of favours stemming from my own acts of magnitude – but I would never ever need any favours: I am an alcoholic – that would be my life and my death.

***

"Irwin, your technical problems are very interesting, but we need an answer – quickly." The immigration official had his job to do.

"This man has been delayed six hours already; just tell me what you can about his iris pattern."

I always find decision-making easy; here they asked me if he was "safe" since they could not classify his iris and the truth is I didn't know. I could not compel the man to have an examination – of any sort other than of his eyes – and he blocked all my queries. I was in checkmate.

"Are the Immigration authorities allowed to enforce further examinations or tests?" I asked.

Mulvey gave a sigh of frustration. "It has never been necessary before, Irwin, and it would take time to get such permission – time we don't have," he added wearily.

"I will speak to him again." I ended with a feigned confidence that, at the very least, sent Mulvey on his way. Could this be the work of some foreign power trying to bypass the immigration identity checks? If this were the case, I could certainly not let the man into our country, but what if…

***

She read the menu with little interest but gave her order with smiles and graciousness which quite surprised me in view of her sulky, taciturnity with me. "You did that very nicely," I said.

"Our waitress has few choices in her life; she tries hard," she replied simply. She *did* know how to change her behaviour!

"Let me move your bag out of the way," I said reaching over. She grabbed at the bag as if protecting it from me and the contents gushed out over the floor; it was full of music manuscript.

"You are a musician!" I said with some enthusiasm. She packed the music back into her case as she replied.

"No, I am not a musician. I taught myself." She stared long and hard at me, "But I do play the flute." She smiled for the first time and drew her flute from her bag, stood up and began to play. The restaurant fell silent. She played like I have never heard music before; it was somehow familiar and yet strange and just totally enchanting.

She finished. The diners, who had all stopped eating during the 'recital,' applauded, somewhat stunned and seemingly as charmed as myself by the performance. She bowed and smiled a most wonderful gracious smile, sat down and reverted to taciturnity.

***

It was actually my day off the next day, so I had really promised Mulvey that I would sort out the problem in my own time; this was tedious, but there was no reason not to drink while "interrogating" the man.

"Petros" – as I was directed to call him was quite open to the idea that he would dine with me that evening as both he and I were stuck with our respective problems. We settled on a good red wine, though we quickly moved onto port and thence to whiskey. The evening rapidly turned into a very pleasant one.

He was certainly a brilliantly informed individual but with some amazing gaps in his knowledge – almost exclusively of trivialities. His delightful smile punctuated our interchanges, and I wondered where I could possibly have seen that smile before. He seemed to get drunk along with me and indeed when we toasted my old medical school, our glasses chinked and smashed. I remember crawling on all fours to sweep up the glass. We laughed. It was a wonderful evening. I learned nothing.

***

"May I ask a question?" I enquired.

"Yes," she sighed with boredom, "just one question and one only," she answered looking at her watch.

"What has made you so unique?"

She looked down and thought for a while. At first, I thought that she wasn't going to answer, then I knew she would. I also had a strange feeling that what she was about to say would change me forever.

***

Mulvey had passed the problem on to his superior. "I must apologise, Irwin," said the boss urbanely, "but I did want to clear this matter up quickly, so I called in Stephan."

Stephan is my "oppo" who does my job for the other three-and-a-half days a week; a man of great charm, a man of great persuasion but above all a man for the quiet life. His decision was totally predictable.

"He said he was also perplexed by his findings, but in view of the overall situation he was happy to leave the problem with you."

I suppressed a smile at the outcome.

"So we can legitimately allow you some more time, though I do hope it will not be necessary to pry unduly or do any of your 'examinations'?" He looked at me, questioningly, seeking my reassurance. I gave a neutral nod. At least I had more time.

***

"My name is Jaquelle," she began, "pronounced Jack-well, with a silent "w" not Jac-kal like the wild dog. My father, who had always admired the English, was hoping to call his son Jack; I was the disappointment, so he feminized his disappointment in the French manner." She smiled; this obviously did not truly bother her. "People have to bear far worse childhoods than mine; anyway I am far stronger and far more intelligent than other children so I can't complain – nor would I wish to." She stated this comment with a dry matter-of-factness.

She wet her lips on her fruit juice; I poured the last of the bottle of wine into my glass.

"About eighteen months ago, my mother took me to the clinic for the results. They are very busy there – very good but very busy. We should have been prepared for some bad news when they called us in ahead of everyone else in the clinic. The consultant looked harassed and tired, and my guess is that she had some problems of her own. She told us to sit down. There was a long silence. Then she looked straight at my mother and said, "Your daughter is dying. We will fight the cancer with our best drugs, but she will be dead long before she reaches her next birthday; in fact, my colleagues all believe that she will be dead within six months. I am so very, very sorry."

She paused for a moment and sipped her drink.

"I have an aunt who lives in the mountains. I asked my mother to let me go there to adjust to the situation. My mother was very understanding; she had seven other children, and through her tears I knew I would not be a great loss to the family."

I could not take my eyes off her beautiful and serene face.

"So I went to my aunt's, picked up a bottle of wine and locked myself in my room with a notebook and some pens and made my plans. I had to cram a lifetime into six months – it was as simple as that."

She folded her serviette.

"When death is imminent you realise how trivial most people's obsessions are. I resolved to discard all the minor themes in life. I made a reading list of all the great works of literature, a list of all the great music I had to listen to. I taught myself to read music, and I taught myself the flute. I sat down with a list of all my friends and scratched through each name one at a time. I truly had no friends that counted in my new reality."

She paused and seemed to notice me for the first time.

"My family are rich and powerful and as they now had no emotional interest in me, they gladly acceded to my modest requests." She paused, "So you see, I have been ready and waiting for death for some 18 months and thus far he has evaded me."

I reached over to her and hugged her; there were tears streaming down my cheeks.

"I would give the world for you to be my daughter," I whispered through my sobs.

***

Twice each day, I visited with Petros and how I enjoyed our conversations; he had a most remarkable mind, a formidable general knowledge, and a certain deep kindness which contrasted sharply with my colleagues. He seemed to know so much of my background, it seemed uncanny. Once, I asked him how he knew so much about me.

"Irwin," he smiled, "you are a very exceptional person with some extra-ordinary qualities; in fact, you are what we might call..." he paused as if in doubt as to whether to continue, "a chosen one," he finally said in a hushed voice.

This meant nothing to me and surely was slippage from the meaning in his native tongue. But Petros truly had the gift of charm. Had the circumstances been different, he would have been my first ever true friend. Yet, I was planning to betray him.

***

We saw each other every day; the pretext was that I was buying her a meal. The more I found out about her, the more beautiful I found her. Each time we met there was something even deeper about her. When she could not come, there was the brown envelope with my name on and a short though gracious note of apology. I realised why I had never been involved with anyone before – their egos, their pettiness, their trivia – but here was someone who had suffered and her soul had been cleansed of pettiness and the egotistical nonsense which dominates so many lives. We spoke on everything; there was nothing between us. It was perhaps three months before I even held her hand – that was the extent of our physicality as I swore in court. These were the happiest days of my life, and I fell in love for the first and only time in my life.

"I will love you always," I said with a tremor in my voice. It was not a promise but a simple statement of fact; fate had thrown a human being to me who was the spirit of the dreams I had not dared to dream.

She stared at the table, "I love you too, Irwin," she said falteringly, "and I didn't want to."

I put my finger on her lips and shook my head. She was too young to say that. Then, somehow, I just didn't need alcohol anymore; it became irrelevant.... I was indeed teetotal!

**

Petros greeted me as warmly as always; he did not know it, but this was to be our final evening together. How sad I felt.

Petros had been my first true friend, and as the wine flowed, I somehow – I still don't know how – found myself revealing things about myself I had never discussed with another living soul.

He listened with particular attention to my story of Jaquelle, and the expression of sadness and concern on his face truly moved me.

"I will see what I can do to help," he said solemnly at the end of my story. I laughed. There was clearly nothing that anyone on earth could do.

As I was about to go, I turned to him and had to make the confession. "Petros, I have betrayed you," I said.

I took out the unopened envelope from my pocket. "My job here is to find out who you are." Petros looked curious.

"Do you remember the first night we ate together and drank some wine? Do you remember that the glasses smashed? Your glass was blue, mine was plain. I took the broken glass, with your lip prints on it and arranged for DNA analysis on the cells adherent to the glass."

He looked totally untroubled by my betrayal.

"Here is the result," I said, holding the envelope up for him to see. Did he look a little saddened then? "Petros, I have become very close to you – like you were my own brother. We must open this envelope together."

Petros looked totally unmoved.

"Do you want to read it first?" I asked. He shook his head and then shrugged his shoulders fatalistically. The report was

118

three pages long with lots of technical jargon which even I could not understand. The summary was, however, quite succinct.

"In this very good sample of cells, we were able to determine that the owner has fifty-two chromosomes and is certainly not human. We have been unable to match any gene sequences with any creature on our database. We can only assume, Irwin, that this has come from some laboratory experiment and congratulate you on this brilliant joke which tested our expertise to the full. I hope this fulfils your wants in this regard and returns, in part, some of the many kindnesses you showed to me in the past." My "friend" who had done the analysis had always regarded me as some sort of wayward genius.

We sat together in silence for a while.

"Petros, I am so sorry but I will have to inform my superiors," I finally said. Petros smiled, wise and with resignation.

"Just give me 24 hours," he requested. I embraced him and left quickly, retiring to a sleepless night.

***

"Today is my birthday," she announced. "We should go away somewhere."

I made a few phone calls and soon we were 'away somewhere' – somewhere so far away it really doesn't matter where. Somewhere so far away from anything I had known before. Yes, then we did spend every moment of every day and night together. The tenderness that shuddered through my being took me through the eye of the needle; the angel rode the beast in love and tenderness and the gates of paradise were flung open to me for the first time.

***

Mulvey stared at the report; he had taken a full 20 minutes to read it.

"Is this some kind of joke, Irwin?" he said with irritation. I explained very slowly and carefully how I had 'stolen' the DNA and secretly had it analysed. I thought he would be impressed.

"Who are we talking about?" he asked.

"Petros Janek of course," I answered with some disbelief. "I have never heard of him," he replied adamantly.

***

Then she disappeared, and I never saw her again. My case at the medical tribunal was a total farce and my suspension for "Paedophilic Behaviour and Alcoholism" was of course absurd, as it was her 19th birthday when we had 'gone away' but there were powerful forces involved; the invocation of religious abuse and racial disrespect all conspired to make the mud stick. I could not even be motivated to fight it properly, or get expert help from my "friends"; I was back drinking with a vengeance. I was a broken man.

Then my medical license was gone. I had no way to make a living. My thoughts were always with Jaquelle. Had her cancer come back? Had her powerful family taken her? Had she just fallen out of love with me?

So that is the story of why I started working for immigration who welcomed my expertise in ophthalmology and shunted me into becoming a super-specialist on the iris!

***

All traces of Petros Janek had been removed; it was as though he had never existed. I went through the files. All gone, erased, removed to the last shred of evidence. I spoke to people who had met Petros; no-one remembered anything. They all seemed totally genuine but how could they forget? Had they all been brainwashed or hypnotised? Nothing made any sense, but one thing was for sure, the slate had somehow been wiped completely clean. Strangely, the worst thing of all was that I really missed Petros. There was a big gap in my life that had only been filled completely once before.

My job continued; I drank half the time and worked the other half. I laughed to myself that, like my beloved Jaquelle, I too was just waiting for the embrace of death.

***

The ambassador was a very skilled communicator.

"We need a sample of your blood," he announced, shrugging his shoulders. "It is all beyond me – political forces at work, methinks. However, they do want to do a paternity check on you, so please Mr Schlebb, please do the right thing."

"A paternity test!" I cried with disbelief, my mind racing. "Of course, I will do my duty – and willingly," I added, "but please may I request that a copy of the report is sent separately to me."

"Yes indeed," said the ambassador, happy to have the request solved so simply. I let them have the sample, but what could this mean? In my entire life I had had but one lover. It could, of course, be a simple mistaken identity, but what if my beloved Jaquelle had had a child? Perhaps her family had insisted on the test? A shudder went down my spine, yet a shudder of joy that she might still be alive and that we could somehow be sharing something else – no matter how remote the possibility. Hope stirred in the depths of my soul.

I waited and wondered how they would let me know. Each morning I went down to the post in hope rather than expectation. I counted the days…

***

First, there was the early morning call from Mulvey.

"So sorry to bother you Irwin, but we have two cases which Stephan could not deal with… he said something about the iris of each of them being quite beyond his experience and would you please have a look." I smiled. Could this be another

Petros? I would go and look but first I checked the post – as I did every day.

And there it was – on the 21st day of waiting – I knew immediately and tore it open impatiently.

"The man under test is indeed the father of the child. The findings are totally unequivocal, having done….."

I was overjoyed; baffled but overjoyed. Nothing could hurt me now. Then I noticed the second envelope. It was addressed to me in a familiar hand; the hand of Jaquelle!!!

My eyes filled with tears as I sat down and reverently opened the envelope. Whatever she wanted of me I would do it. It read:

My Dear Irwin,

As you can see from the address, I am now living in a refugee camp and I am quite safe. My escape from my family and from my "arranged" marriage was quite exciting and I think you would be proud of me, though I could not have managed it without the help of a total stranger who said he was a friend of yours! I knew this was wrong as you have never had any friends. His name is Petros Janek and he is the most courageous and kind person I have ever met; he accompanied me to the camp and even now he is making the camp a better place. He said to tell you: "We have come to help." Anyway, you may well have married yourself since I have not seen you for so long and if so you must ignore this letter completely. I write simply to reassure you that your son and I remain well and that I still love you. There is nothing else to say. I bless you for now and the future,

All my love,

Jaquelle

I stood for a long time, the envelope clutched to my chest, tears pouring down my cheeks. How clearly I knew what had to be done. I knew what I had to do with Mulvey's problem clients, but above all, I knew with a total and absolute certainty I had never known that I must get her back. Yes, it was time to call in a few more favours and make things happen. Then with Jaquelle at my side, nothing else mattered to me, and I would never drink again.

The Cougar

I was born a city boy; more particularly, I was born a slum boy - a slum where I belonged, a slum in which I wallowed, a slum in which I thrived. I was happy there, surrounded as I was by friends and allies so that the stench, the filth, and the discomfort were barely registered in my consciousness. I also had my best friend, my ally, my "Big Brother" Ryan.

He would always watch my back. He was always a step ahead in planning what to do next; he had a "jungle sense," and a creative ingenuity which meant that none of us ghetto kids, us white-trash, died, got injured or ended up in prison. Ryan was the only true genius I've ever met; he was my guardian angel and my best friend.

"Can you ride a bike?" he asked, one day, looking up from a crumpled old map.

"Of course," I lied, never wishing to lose face with him, "it's easy."

Ryan continued to pore over the map.

"Okay. Tomorrow, Tobin's yard, about this time, just you and me."

And that is how it all started.

***

He gave me the girl's bike, which should have been easier to ride and was quite amused by my eager ineptness and my several falls en route to mastering the art. Even so, in just a few hours, we were out in the suburbs and I was totally, totally lost.

"Nearly halfway there," smiled Ryan. My legs were aching from the unaccustomed exercise, but there was no point in complaining to Ryan; he never acknowledged pain himself, and he expected the same from us.

***

By now we were ravenously hungry, but I never worried when I was with Ryan; he would always think of something. We parked the bikes discreetly in some bushes, and I followed Ryan into the supermarket.

"Would you get me the boss please?" he smiled at the girl on the counter. She looked puzzled.

"Is he expecting you?" she asked looking a little suspicious.

Ryan had one of those smiles that could open a can of beans, and he used it now.

"He will be very happy to see me as we haven't seen each other for months."

Soon a young man appeared looking rather flustered and who obviously had things on his mind. Ryan flashed a smile again and briefly explained to the boss that the two of us were on our way to Calabogie to visit a sick uncle and we had no food. He had noticed that the car park was full of litter and that we would be happy to clean up the whole area in exchange for any food which had passed its sell-by date. If I had not seen Ryan in action before, I would have been surprised how quickly he gained the result.

We worked with enthusiasm and the job took less than an hour. Soon we were eating some fruit and sandwiches, and we would have plenty spare for the rest of the journey. The boss seemed to warm to us, and after some pleasantries, Ryan gave me a subtle kick under the table, which meant that he was up to something and I should play along. "Sir, I was talking to my friend earlier about the magic of palmistry, and you could help settle an argument here… if I may?" Ryan stepped forward and gazed into the palms of the boss. He began speaking, slowly and thoughtfully at first, then with some concerns and suggestions. After about ten minutes, the man was clearly deeply moved by the "revelations."

Ryan gazed into space for a few very long seconds:

"… so you have to balance the hurt you'll cause, against following that sacred love in your life. It's a tough call, but you can do it… I know that deep down you have the strength to do the right thing," he paused and closed his eyes, "… and delay, delay brother, is the very worst, the *very* worst… delay gives nothing but pain, brother."

The man stared at his hands with tears pouring down his face. We waited in silence.

"Boys, please call again on your way back…" He took out a $10 bill and put it into Ryan's hand. Ryan signalled we should go.

And that was the magic of Ryan. I have never known anyone who could read people so well; he could tell the man was troubled and made a guess that there were personal dilemmas in his life. He always seemed able to tap into what people needed to know. Ryan was a genius, and I owed my survival to him.

***

"Where are we going, by the way?" I finally asked.

"Calabogie," he replied. I was none the wiser.

We carried on for some more hours. I was tired and thirsty, but you never mentioned such things to Ryan; it was our code of honour.

***

When the footpaths began to peter out, we hid the bikes in some bushes. "They are safe there," said Ryan after checking their hiding place from several directions.

We walked for perhaps a half hour further, with Ryan occasionally looking at his compass. Finally, we came upon a ramshackle "dwelling-place" and Ryan removed a key from his pocket. He didn't need it; the door was open. Ryan looked delighted even though the furnishings were rudimentary. "This will be a good base," he announced.

We had some more food and drink, and I quickly collapsed into an exhausted sleep.

***

When I finally awakened, the place was transformed and certainly habitable; Ryan had even managed to rig up a small gas lamp. However, the insects were biting and a real nuisance.

"Let's get away from these insects," he said, turning off the lamp.

Outside, the sun was quickly setting, and the full moon was on the rise. Ryan stopped and made himself comfortable looking down on a quiet stream; I did the same. Soon Ryan was asleep, but I was wide awake. What was this place with no rumble of traffic, with no noises of the city? This was a mystical silence, punctuated only by the clicks and whirrs of insects, the occasional sounds of night birds, whooping and calling, and other sounds that I could not even classify... friends or foes I knew not. I was unafraid, just totally alert to every sound and every sight, to every hush and every shadow. I felt a blissful harmony with myself and the world for the first time in my life. Thus I remained for perhaps an hour or two, who knows. By now the sun had set, and the moon threw cloaks of blackness over the bushes; then it happened.

***

First, there was a soft mewing sound; it was very quiet but sounded so near. Then, I saw the eyes, the most beautiful lonely eyes I have ever seen. It looked up at the moon and sniffed the air, alert and so majestically alone. Silently, it moved to the stream and began to drink. I could scarcely breathe, and my heart was pounding so loud in my chest I was certain it would hear me. I was afraid to blink even, in case I broke the magic spell of the moment; time stood still. Finally, I remembered Ryan and realised that I must share this with him; I reached over and softly shook his shoulder. He

127

stirred and the cat was gone. And that was it; the minute that changed my life was over.

***

Back in the shack, I could scarcely contain my feelings, and the words just came tumbling out. Ryan smiled.

"Perhaps you just imagined it," he shrugged. I was furious and protested indignantly that I had seen something very, very real indeed. He calmed me down and had me describe in great detail the creature I had seen.

"Okay, you didn't imagine it," he said looking up at me, "you did see a creature and from your description it was a mountain lion - a cougar... but I cannot understand all your excitement, after all it is only a dumb animal!" A red mist came down before my eyes and I grabbed his collar in indignation.

"A dumb animal, a dumb animal, she is the most beautiful thing I have ever seen," I said tightening my hold. Ryan laughed and easily broke my grip.

"Okay, okay little brother, tonight we will go together and see your mysterious creature!"

***

The whole of the next night we waited patiently for her to appear, but nothing happened. I was devastated; such a wonderful experience needs to be shared, and the "failure" left me feeling hollow inside. I begged Ryan to come with me one further night, and reluctantly he agreed. Then, at the same time as the night before, shortly after the sun had set, we were rewarded. She shone like silver in the moonlight, and I swear that she looked at me as before, deep into my eyes, and I know that Ryan had the same experience. We walked back in silence, trembling from what had happened.

***

From then on, each weekend we would go to the woods together, and the cougar became a bond between us; we saw her several times and each time the experience seemed even greater than the one before. We tried to tell the other members of the gang but soon realised it was useless; you had to see the cougar yourself or you would never, you *could* never, understand.

Then came the fateful weekend when Ryan could not come with me to the woods. He was a little uneasy about my going alone, but there was nothing to be done. I had no choice.

This time she did not appear, but I heard a cry from deep in the woods; could this be her? Slowly, silently I followed the mysterious cry. I have seen many horrific sights in my life, but nothing chilled me to my very core as seeing my beloved cougar with her leg caught in a trap. I froze in horror, and then as I inched forward, she snarled at me and surely would have attacked. I sat and waited for a long time and then very slowly moved towards her and, with some difficulty, removed the trap from her leg; she could have killed me at any moment, but she surely knew that I would rather die than hurt her. She looked at me for perhaps 20 seconds, moved off and quickly disappeared into the shadows. That look she had given me – of her lonely magnificence – burned into my soul and would stay there forever.

***

At first, the other kids seemed rather bored with my talk as I gave them the facts about mountain lions, but when I began to relate my own experiences, they fell totally silent and I could feel their eyes glued to my face. The buzzer sounded to end my presentation, but Mr Curran, our teacher, bade me carry on. I finally finished, my heart so full of re-living my experiences with the cougar that I scarcely noticed the reaction of the class.

"That was outstanding," said Mr Curran. He looked down and paused for a while before dismissing the rest of the kids. He was silent for a while and then said:

"Remember, Fratellino, that to help the things you care about, you need to achieve, you need to do well at school. *If* and I mean *if...*" he said looking very serious, "...if you really love that creature, you will be able to help it more by having the power of a successful education. These cats are in danger, and a person like you with a good education behind him could make a difference." He held my gaze for another long minute.

"You are a good kid and the power of your love can make things happen. Do you understand me?"

But I had understood very well indeed. I knew what had to be done and indeed my education took a sharp turn for the better.

***

My passion for the cougar continued, and I saw her several times after "the incident." I even began to believe that she really did know me. Even when I was abroad in the Army, my thoughts were always in those magical woods. I volunteered for specialist training and became a sniper and a woodsman, these skills bringing me closer to her. I learned about survival in the woods, about animal traps (and how to break them), and about every aspect of hunting (and what could go wrong in the woods). I shared the cougar with no one, for only Ryan would have understood.

***

He looked down at my injuries as I lay on the hospital bed.

"Ryan! Are you a colonel, now?" Not that I was surprised by the sudden appearance of my 'big brother' – he was the sort of person who could appear anywhere, anytime.

"Not really," he smiled enigmatically. "I am very useful to a lot of people," he added almost apologetically.

"Have you seen her?" he asked. I nodded and explained the various encounters we had made. He smiled happily, and I felt sure that she was almost as important in his life as in mine. We sat in silence for a while. He looked again at my injuries:

"You will be fine, though you will always have a limp…. the same limp as her's," he added shaking his head in some amusement.

"Nurse," he called, "bring me this man's chart, he is still in some pain." He wrote on the chart; the nurse gave me an injection. When I awoke, he was gone. That was the last time I saw Ryan until many years later when he came to stay with me in the woods.

***

But now I am old, old and at peace with my past and my memories. My wife has long-since died, and my son lives abroad. I live alone in the woods like my beloved cougar, in my simple, remote shack, with everything I could possibly want. By day, I wander silently looking for her tell-tale paw prints in the wet clay by the streams; by night I listen for the mews and cries that tell me she lives on. The hunters no longer come to her woods; a succession of very unhappy hunting accidents had her woods re-Christened "The Haunted Woods."

They tried to trap her, but they were amateurs and me, her defender, a professional, so they finally gave up. Sometimes I see her, just for a few seconds as her eyes flash in the moonlight or maybe just a silver blur in the shadows and my heart skips a beat, a beat like the very first time I beheld her face. I know that I will spend the rest of my days in the kingdom of my beloved; it is where I belong.

True Love

I cannot imagine not loving Alfie. I truly believe that I was born loving him. There are lots of twins around, of course, but none of them are like Alfie and me – they have spats and disagreements and are capable of falling out and drifting apart – but not us. We were always a team – a force. Being orphans brings twins even closer together, but though I have spoken with many others in the same situation, there can be no doubt that Alfie and I were way beyond all extremes of bond and feeling; we were magic together.

Thinking about this, I should perhaps say that Alfie was sunshine in human form; his smile would melt a glacier and somehow whatever he did, reciting poetry or singing in front of the class, made all the children smile and be happy. When God gave out talent, beauty, and charm, he gave it all to Alfie and I rejoice in him and don't begrudge that I was left with the dregs. We are after all a single unit.

***

Then an angel came to visit the orphanage; they didn't tell us what it was for – but I knew: this angel and her husband wanted to adopt one of us.

She was the most beautiful creature I had ever seen, and after her first appearance I dreamed of having her for our mother; our own kitchen, our very own room, our own home and the love of this beautiful, tender person who radiated love and gentleness. I know she wanted us both; I even overheard her arguing with her husband, but he was adamant – it was me or Alfie!

Perhaps I just valued Alfie's happiness beyond my own – and, of course, that is true, and I know that if I had left Alfie in the orphanage and I had been chosen, I could not have borne the pain, thinking of him alone and abandoned. For whatever reason, the embarrassment of a nine-year-old as the warm urine wet his trousers and spilt upon the floor was not to be

ignored; had there been a choice to be made, I had certainly
made it for them.

***

We didn't do tears in the orphanage, just a hug and a smile,
me being so happy that Alfie had a beautiful home and a real
mother of his own. I stood on the steps and waved as the
huge car drove off.

***

The first day seemed like a month; the orphanage seemed like
a tomb without him; the children forgot to smile. The pain of
loss within my chest made me wonder how I could survive,
but I had a burning conviction that I would see him soon –
just like the sun rose in the mornings – an inevitability. Could
they not see how much I was suffering? It was beyond the
realms of possibility that they could keep us apart. A week
went by, then two weeks, then a month and nothing; no
word, no sign. I was beyond desperation.

***

It was easy to go missing on Saturdays, so I did. I just walked
and walked. Destiny would surely smile on me and take me to
Alfie as no God could let a creature suffer so much pain.
When it grew dark, I realised how hungry I was. I climbed
over the railings of a park and found a drinking fountain. In
spite of my hunger, I fell asleep on a bench.

In the morning, the hunger was raging even more, and I sifted
through rubbish bins for scraps; they tasted wonderful. I
continued walking, in absolute certainty that I would find
him, though I felt weak and faint.

***

I didn't mean to steal the food at the café; I was sure it was a
leftover.

"What's your name?" asked the policeman?

"Alfonso Higgins," I whispered. The policeman smiled.

"We have all been looking for you; you have created quite a stir!" he said.

I never spoke much in those days, but in his car, after a whole bar of chocolate, I did tell the nice policeman about Alfie and why I had gone to find him.

***

"...and make sure that Alfonso gets to see his brother or he will wander off again... he is a very strong-willed young man." The policeman made it very clear to the orphanage what their responsibilities were.

***

And so I got to see Alfie every week in his beautiful big house; these were such happy times. He told me about his mother and everything she said, about the wonderful things she cooked and their trips out in the car. He showed me his school uniform and talked about his new school; it sounded so amazing, I resolved to visit him there.

***

I am a very quick runner, and though the school was a few miles from my own, I set off in my lunch break, arriving breathless and sweaty. The school yard was full of beautiful children, all dressed in their maroon uniforms.

I chose the most impressive big boy I could find.

"Do you know a new boy called Alfie?" I asked.

"You mean the sissy little blond kid?" he replied. No-one had ever, ever insulted Alfie before and a red mist came down. Before I knew what was happening, I had grabbed him by the throat and dragged him to the ground. But he was a lot bigger than me and soon was sitting on me hitting me in the face. The fight was broken up by an irate school-teacher, furious with me. He sent me on my way, warning me never to come near the school again. I felt injured and vengeful.

***

It was an amazing place called "Paraclete" – a rambling second-hand bookstore with a strange "bookie" smell and an impression of organised chaos.

"What are you looking for, son?" asked Mr Paraclete, a small, wiry, wrinkled old man with dyed green hair. I thought for a minute, then risked everything.

"I want to learn how to kill a man," I finally said.

Mr Paraclete laughed, especially when he discovered I had no money. Nonetheless, he quickly showed me some books on self-defence; I was intrigued and began reading through them. One of them stood out. "How much is this?" I asked. He laughed again, pointing out that I could not buy it without any money. Finally, he smiled and said I could have the book if I cleaned his car. I could not believe it! This was an opportunity to learn skills that might protect my beloved Alfie, and I set to work with a passion.

***

"That is the cleanest my car has ever been!" he exclaimed. "You can have the book and also a drink."

Maybe he was lonely, but he talked to me for several hours about his life, his lost son and his love of books. "You can learn anything from books," he said. He was almost curt with the customers who interrupted our conversation, and in retrospect, the whiskey he was putting in his tea was making him rather drunk. He gave me some, and though I didn't like the taste, I drank it from politeness and began to talk myself.

The outcome was spectacular for me. He thought I was a 'smart kid' (no-one had ever said that to me before, or any compliment for that matter) and if I would work with him every Saturday he would pay me to clean his car and for every book I sold! Unfortunately, he would have to pay me in books as he was 'not a very rich man.'

***

And so I became a "bookworm," but a very particular sort of bookworm; I had no interest in fiction, but a total passion for learning how to do things. I found that you can learn just about anything from a book. There were even books on magic! Mr Paraclete talked to me a lot, often repeating stories, but he was very experienced in the world and optimistic that there was always some way around any problem you come across, and the answer was almost always in a book.

***

But Alfie had taken a turn for the worse; he had been bullied at school and had started to get bad headaches. He seemed so sad; I was beside myself on what to do. The main bully was a boy called Briggs who made life at school very difficult for Alfie.

"Do you want me to kill him for you?" I asked innocently; and if he had said the word, then I truly would have done it. But maybe there would be another way to solve the problem.

***

My Saturday mornings went from strength to strength. It seems hard to believe that by doing such obvious things my life improved so much. I read books on how to sell things, but soon surpassed what they taught me, using my 'orphan status' and magic tricks to engage with the customers; I even learned to read palms (from a book of course!) and the rudiments of humour. Mr Paraclete was delighted, as people were coming to his shop just to see me, though he did resent the claims on our "conversation time" which allowed him to repeat his stories again and again! The shop really did become more successful and he started paying me in cash – not much, but enough for me to buy a rusty old bike so I could visit Alfie whenever I wished.

***

Alfie spoke to me a lot about his headaches and his fear of school; there was even some talk of him having his own private teacher at home! I tried to cheer him by talking about the shop and how I had increased sales with magic tricks. For once, Alfie looked interested, and when I did him some magic – even simple tricks with coins or matches – the old joy came rushing back to his face. I went back to my magic studies with a vengeance and every time I went to see him I had a new trick, usually with some funny stories to make him smile. I know he enjoyed my visits and so did his mother… those were some of the happiest days of my life. I remember one day his mother put her arm around me and kissed me on the back of my head; I smelt her perfume and felt her breasts against my shoulder and I tried to dash the strange longings that surged inside me for my priority was to fix the Briggs problem! I would have to go back to the school and confront him.

**

It is just about commitment; when you need to do something, you live, eat and sleep the problem until it yields to you. I had to find out everything about Briggs, and I did, using every technique there was. I had to prepare for my school visit and so I would not be recognised, I dyed my hair blond and put on a very convincing false moustache – a big, black droopy thing which made Alfie laugh. I researched everything I needed to know and set the date.

**

The children arrived at the school to see a strange tent in the playing field; they swarmed around to investigate and Briggs was at the front.

Suddenly there was a clap of thunder and the magician, with blond hair and a black droopy moustache appeared from no-where. They were all taken aback, but Briggs led the applause. I put on the best show I have ever done in the seven minutes I had allowed for; then with their total attention fixed, I drew a veil over my head and spoke in the sombre "Satan Voice" I had practised to perfection.

"There is a message from the other world for one amongst you, and it is very urgent for him." I then went on to reveal the many personal details about Briggs which I had researched, including his "sin" of bullying Alfie, finally announcing that his soul had been marked by the forces of evil and they would be coming for him soon... unless... unless he undid the harm that he had done. I could see from behind the veil that Briggs was white with fear.

"But what should I do?" he whimpered.

"I will implore of the heavens," I intoned, reaching my arms up to the sky. A huge scroll appeared magically in my upturned hands. "You must follow these instructions to the letter or your fate is sealed." I stared deep into his eyes and I knew the job was done.

A bell rang, the children scampered off to class, and I packed away the tent.

***

But the problem had not gone away. True that Briggs had gone to the house at the time specified on the scroll, and had sworn to protect Alfie when he returned to school, but the headaches persisted and Alfie did not go back to school. He spoke a lot about his headaches and his suffering and the only way I could distract him was with magic tricks and funny stories. My heart still ached when I saw his beautiful face, but he spent much of his time in bed and was becoming quite plump whereas I was skinny and always hungry from all the calories I burned up bicycling around. What else could I do to save him? He was so much more sensitive and tender than me that I would die to help him; in spite of everything he was not happy.

***

Then it was our 16th birthdays, and they organised a party for Alfie at their big house. Some of the kids from the orphanage came too and made themselves ill on the sumptuous food. Even here Alfie seemed despondent and went off early to bed with another headache. The rest of us sang and danced and had a wonderful time; I even had a dance with Alfie's mother and everyone laughed hysterically as she tried (unsuccessfully!) to teach me the waltz. I just felt so sorry that Alfie had been too sick to enjoy his own party!

***

For the next couple of years, I went to see Alfie as often as I could, always hoping that things would change. His mother would always welcome me with genuine joy whenever I arrived and watched my magic and jokes with obvious delight.

Then one evening, and I don't know quite know how it happened, I read her palm. I can scarcely remember what I said, just some of the stock phrases from the book, but going "off script" and following my intuition as I had done so many times before. I vaguely remember talking about her suffering and how I would love to be the one to help her.

I do remember that, after it, her eyes filled with tears and she looked into my eyes and said. "I think you are the one." I had no idea what it meant.

***

The weather closed in shortly after that with much snow and ice; it was out of the question to ride my bike to Alfie's. Then there was a break in the weather, and I managed to get there. They were so pleased to see me – even more than usual and his mother "insisted" that she take me home in her car. She said she wanted to talk to me and with some strange electric key made the park gates open for the car and then shut behind us. It was blank darkness; we were alone. She began to speak, something about wanting children and her husband Sam said it was okay... I did not understand and was probably not listening as first she held my hand and drew me to her, then put my hand on her breast. I could smell her wondrous perfume and felt my own hand slide around her waist as I hugged her towards me. The seats seemed to slide backwards on their own, and her hand slid nervously to my groin. I had never kissed a woman before, but this kiss welled up from the very pits of my being. I began to kiss her breasts with an abandonment that astonished me and with her expert help I first explored her femaleness and then entered her. She began to coo strange noises, and at first I feared that she was in pain.

"I would never hurt you – never," I said, but she was obviously happy to be so close to me. I stayed inside her for so long and I truly wanted it to last forever.

"That was beautiful," she said as she dropped me off at my doorstep.

***

For three months I had everything; with transport provided by Alfie's mother, Emma, I could see him as often as I wanted – which was nearly every night. On the way home, Emma and I would be lovers – true, beautiful lovers. I read as much as I could about sex and put it all into practice; what could be more fulfilling than giving pleasure to a person you adore. And I truly did adore Emma, and I know that she knew it, though when she asked: "Do you love me, Alphonso?" I had to tell her that though I had an intense fondness for her, my deepest love and loyalties were for Alfie... I think she understood.

***

"Congratulations, Alphonso, you are going to become a father," she told me with some sadness.

"Isn't that what you wanted?" I asked, rather puzzled.

"Yes, Sam and I wanted a child of our own, but now I have no excuse to see you anymore." She looked into my eyes through her tears. "And I will miss you... tomorrow I will tell Sam, and that will be the end of it."

We made love for the last time; the finality and desperation of it all made it even more exquisite than before, as two lost souls said their goodbyes under the stars.

I still saw Alfie – that goes without saying – but I found it harder than ever to make him smile. He smoked cigarettes non-stop, and I could not stay too long as I began to choke on the fumes. He had also started having some injections from the doctor which interrupted my visits, and he really did not look very well at all. I saw Emma occasionally and when I did a strange sadness tore into my heart...

***

They called the baby "Alph" and showed him off to everyone; he was quite beautiful. The proud couple had their fulfilment now, and my discretion was, of course, total unto death.

***

I never lost hope that Alfie would be well someday; after all, he had the best of everything – wonderful care from excellent nurses and expensive doctors. Yet he continued to decline, and when the end came, his death still hit me like a mortal blow. I locked myself alone in my room for a long time; it was a grief I could share with no-one. But there it was. I left my grief in my room, for now I had people who depended on me and life had to go on.

***

I held my son's hand as we walked from the grave.

"Did you love my brother, Alfie?" He was very smart and direct for a seven-year-old.

"Yes, more than anyone I have ever loved!"

We walked awhile in silence.

"Hopefully, you will grow up to be like him someday," I added.

Alph stopped and looked up into my eyes.

"It is you I want to be like. You are the one."

A boy and his father looked into each other's eyes for a long time, and it seemed that the boy perhaps understood a dark and beautiful secret that he could not yet comprehend.

The Tunnel

(Dedicated to the memory of Melissa)

The valley was dying. Each day the signs became worse. Each day the sun became fainter behind the clouds of gas. Each day the grass became browner and more lifeless until the earth was laid bare. In that shadowed valley, the cold crept in minute by minute. It had been many months since the last bird sung. Any hope of spring was long since gone; the valley was in its final death-throes.

Valda looked at her reflection in the water. She had changed. The valley had taken its toll. Her skin, her eyes and the faint blueness on her lips, all told the same story. She had delayed facing the inevitable but the time had arrived. She must escape through the tunnel, and it must be now.

How often had she thought about her escape? How often had she rehearsed and prepared for the terrors that lay in wait? Only some could she know; others were just the stuff of nightmares. The measurements and checks were complete, and every item in her satchel had been scrutinised by those who had gone before.

She took a big breath and walked into the overhang which led to the tunnel. She took the large purple pill as she had been instructed, and soon in the mistiness which followed, she walked to the gates. She donned the tunnel-helmet with its special tunnel-illuminator and struggled into the tightly-fitting body supporter and squeezed its grips. She felt lighter. She pulled back the shutters and then opened the iron portals. She walked in. The doors clanged behind her. She stood alone in the darkness; there was no turning back.

***

In the tunnel, all was black, and at first, it was totally silent. Valda waited; she waited so that her eyes could become accustomed to the blackness. Then, she turned on the illuminator in her helmet and began to walk forward. Strange shadows and shapes flickered, tricks of her mind maybe, but anything might happen in the tunnel. Her ears too became accustomed to the silence, and soon she began to notice strange noises; scratching and slithering noises mostly in the distance but some quite close by.

"Watch the floor. Do not rush," she recited from the Catechism of her instructions as she slowly stepped onto the first stairway. Even noises close by did not distract her as she held her gaze downwards. Suddenly she felt the draft from the wings of some powerful bird as it beat against her cheek and quickly flew off having stolen something from the open satchel. She froze and raised her head; the illuminator spotlighted a small but very beautiful owl. For a moment she was in horror, thinking that something vital might have been taken from her satchel; then she remembered: "The Owl is your friend. Always leave your satchel opened." She must stick to the basics, and then at least she could avoid some of the bigger dangers.

The staircase became more and more steep, and in the dark it would have been so easy to fall were she wearing shoes; however, a law of the tunnel was 'always walk in bare feet' and how useful that now turned out to be. She felt every change in texture, every shift in gradient, as she became totally attuned to the feel of the darkness. Nonetheless, when the staircase levelled out onto a short landing, it came as a great relief. Here she could relax and take stock.

She lifted her head into the blackness and froze. Less than ten feet away was the monster of her nightmares; it was the Black Rat! She stared in terror at the loathsome creature. This had been the focus of her nightmares for so many years, and now she was to confront it. Yet the rat looked at her with some disinterest; it certainly was not ready to attack her. It just seemed to be biding its time.

She squeezed hard on the grips of the supportor. Again, she felt the draft from some powerful wings and a huge owl flew menacingly at The Rat which responded by shambling off into the distance. "The Owl is your friend," she remembered. This must indeed be "The Great Owl" which had been foretold in her training. If only she could tell what The Great Owl were thinking, but He remained totally un-readable.

The stairs began again, this time even steeper. She moved on slowly; it was important not to rush. Things take as long as they take in a situation like this. "Watch the floor! Do not rush!" she kept telling herself.

The staircase now felt hard and rocky, and her feet were becoming bruised by some hard stones, but she knew that she must always be aware of the texture of the floor under her feet; that was how you survived the tunnel, sensing the floor at all times – shoes would mean death. She started as she heard a flurry of wings beating, brushing against her face. Instinctively, she lifted her arms to fend away what was attacking her, but from long rehearsals kept her feet rooted to the floor while she did it. The light showed that they were bats, tiny bats, which looked almost green in the dim light.

She raised her hand to fend them off, but they were too quick, darting in and biting into her flesh. Somehow the bites did not hurt, and she instinctively knew that the bats were not real enemies. After what seemed like ages, the staircase levelled out. She stood still and looked up; sure enough, The Great Owl was still there, focussed and inscrutable.

She looked down again, firmly hanging onto the grips for support. In front of her was a huge hole; if she had carried on walking, she would have plummeted to her death. Slowly, she moved around its edge. It seemed to stretch from one wall of the tunnel right to the other side; it seemed impassable! She explored her side of the hole for several minutes before she noticed some steps leading downwards. There was nothing to hang onto, and they looked fairly unsafe. However, there was no choice. Trembling, she stepped down into its depths.

One step at a time, establishing balance at each step before venturing further, down she went. She counted the steps. There were 273. The floor then levelled out, and straight in front of her was The Black Rat. It did not look as though it was going to attack, nor was there any emotion in its eyes; it just looked as though it owned her.

She stared at it for several minutes, composing herself and aware of the terror thudding into her chest. For many years, her fear of The Rat had been lurking in the depths of her mind, but now there was no choice. The Rat was blocking her way, and she must force her way past. Just before she could move, however, she felt the beating of wings and felt something happening to her satchel; the little owl had put something in there. She groped around in the satchel; it was a tiny bottle filled with fluid. "You must always trust the owls," she had heard so many times. She drank the fluid. After a few moments, The Rat snarled at her and moved off. She shone a light on the floor to ensure that there were no other dangers and then continued.

***

She moved on timidly and cautiously, sliding one foot in front of the other. The floor was now wet and cold, and it seemed almost alive under her bruised feet. Although progress was slow, Valda gained in confidence, as she had been told that the first few hours in the tunnel were often the most difficult. How far she had descended through this tunnel she dared not think, and anyway going back was not an option.

She began to hear the sound of running water, and as she slowly inched forward, the sounds became louder and louder. It was a fast flowing stream - but how deep and how wide? Even her illuminator could not see to the other side of the stream, yet this was the only way forward. She would have to swim or at least wade through the waters.

Valda balanced her supportor and put her toe into the stream; it was icy cold. This was the moment she would have to let go of her supportor and strike out into the water. Was this the final moment of truth? Could she survive without her supportor? She fastened her satchel, adjusted her illuminator and, ready to embrace death, jumped into the water.

***

How long she had been unconscious she had no idea – a
second, a minute, an hour? She 'awoke' to find herself
swimming; a slow, graceful breaststroke through the frozen
waters. She looked around; everything was total blackness.
Then she noticed the ripples just to her right and behind her.
She strained her head to see what it was and shuddered as she
saw The Black Rat. It looked fixedly ahead as though it had
just been deprived of a meal. Then, overhead, appeared The
Great Owl. It feigned to attack The Black Rat, which instantly
disappeared, diving deeper into the icy waters.

She swam, almost unaware of the pain from her aching limbs
until she saw the bank. Then her light went out, and there
were deafening incomprehensible noises. As her light
flickered on and off, she saw The Black Rat waiting on the
bank, smacking its lips. Each time the light went out, it felt
that it would never return, though it was probably just a
flicker in real time. The Little Owl was always fluttering
around her, diving into her satchel, whether to leave items
there or to take objects away, but it was reassuring to have it
around. Finally, the light came back on and stayed on. The
Great Owl appeared and swooped onto The Rat which
squealed and ran off into the shadows, but she knew it would
not go away and would be lying in wait further down the
tunnel.

Totally exhausted, she hauled herself out of the black waters
and onto the bank. Yet she still felt a total terror without her
supportor. How could she live without it? Then she spied it: a
new supportor – slightly different in shape and size, but
nonetheless, a supportor. She frantically squeezed herself into
it and clung for dear life to the small grips. So she stayed,
numbed by cold and fear, until she found the strength and
courage to move on.

'Surely now the worst was over?' she prayed to herself. Very
soon she came to a sloping path which wound upwards as if
to a high attic. The pathway became increasingly steep, and

even though she went very slowly and cautiously, she became quite breathless. Strange flying creatures which she could not define in the darkness kept brushing against her face, making low-pitched moaning noises. "Show no anger," she cried aloud, trying not to break another rule.

She walked up the staircase and could feel the cold engulfing her more and more. Soon her teeth began to chatter and she knew that the cold was a real danger. She stopped and opened her satchel. She groped in the bottom and, sure enough, there was a cloak for which she had hoped. She put it around her. After a few minutes, she felt far warmer and strangely cheered; the satchel had been well-prepared. "Always check the satchel in times of danger," she recited from her rehearsed catechism.

Higher and higher she went, and now there was a dim light surrounding her, although where it came from she had no idea. The light was reflected between the pillars of ice with their strange carvings – strange shapes which she had never seen before and yet which were somehow familiar. Breathless from the climb, the warm air from her lungs hung like clouds in this temple of ice. She was very, very dry and thirsty after the climb, and broke off a thick icicle and greedily sucked it. That was always the plan: "Check what you can, then trust with all your heart," she recited to herself. She looked up. The Great Owl gazed silently down on her.

Then suddenly her feet almost went from under her; she was standing on sheer black ice. The Little Owl was frantic and dropped a container into her satchel. Holding on for dear life with one hand, she snatched it up, tore off the top and began to drink. It was the most sumptuous drink she could ever remember; it seemed to flow everywhere in her body bringing glowing warmth. Even her feet became warmer, and the ice under them seemed to melt, gradually improving the grip of her toes. She cautiously moved on up the ever-steepening trail, holding on to the grips and watching the floor for any sign of danger.

Noises were everywhere, noises from strange flying creatures that seemed to scratch at her face – like gnats irritating and chafing at her. Finally, she lost control, lifted her head up and tried to swat some of them. They were like small, green flying lizards and as her hand made contact with them, they exploded in a puff of smoke which she could not help but inhale. The smoke – a fine powder – made her choke and she had to stay still, coughing and spluttering. She was sure that she was going to choke to death; it served her right as she had broken the rule of always watching the floor. Finally, the Little Owl managed to fly through the cloud and dropped something into her satchel; she reached for it in desperation. It was a small, liquid-filled pump. In anguish, she discharged its contents into the cloud; almost immediately her choking sensations began to ease, and in just a few minutes the cloud began to disperse.

She continued up the slope, still very breathless from inhaling the toxic powder. Although she stopped from time to time, she felt quite light-headed. The blue, faint mist that seemed to engulf her might have been part of her dizziness or may have been real; reality and imaginings were becoming increasingly blurred. White shapes danced in front of her eyes and strange noises – strange threatening noises – came from above.

However, the rules were exactly the same: "Watch your feet, check what you can, trust the rest. In an emergency, the satchel is prepared." She continued slowly upwards, trying to ignore the bizarre apparitions.

The stairs seemed to go on for ages, and even the air seemed thinner and harder to breathe. Finally, the steps levelled out onto an eerie landing area. She stopped, gasping from the climb, and peered around her. The only way forward was a bridge made of flimsy-looking ropes. She tested it, and even though unsure that it would support her, there was obviously no choice as this was the only way forward. She needed extra vision for this challenge and fished around in her satchel for her accessory torch; she held it in her mouth as she dared not let go of the bridge's handrails. She stepped one cautious step at a time along the rope bridge. The bats were vexing and noisy but she tried to ignore them, and though progress was slow, and she had to stop several times to regain her balance, she finally made it to the other side.

Here, there was a ledge, just wide enough for one person; it stretched across her path. She carefully balanced her new supportor and began to edge around it to the right until she could go no further. The ledge just stopped, straight in front of the rock face. Disappointed, she retraced the steps and went back the other way. Again, this came to a sheer rock face. A wave of despair came over her. "Never lose your Faith," she intoned from the catechism. She began to edge back the way she had come. Then she noticed that the rock face was not unbroken, but that a huge boulder blocked the exit.

It really did look hopeless; the boulder must weigh several tons, and there was no way she could budge it. What to do? Despair engulfed her as there seemed no way out. Then she remembered what she had been told: "Things are not what they seem in the tunnel; choose a belief that works for you." She made her decisions and walked straight at the boulder, just watching her feet and focusing on the floor. There was a noise of rushing winds in her ears and she felt as if she were accelerating at great speed. Finally, she stopped and looked around her, keeping her feet rooted to the ground. She looked behind her; there was the boulder, still completely blocking the path.

**

She walked on slowly, with the illuminator focused on the ground. There was The Black Rat once again, but this time it looked a lot smaller; she ignored it, walked right through it and carried on. Valda was learning quickly.

The tunnel began to slope upwards once more, and the climb became more and more difficult, but taking it one step at a time, her progress continued. Then the tunnel opened up into a huge cavern and the noises began anew, terrifying, deafening noises. Her grip on the supportor tightened as she looked for an escape. Her heart was pounding, and this seemed to be the very worst part of all. After everything she had been through, would this all be in vain? There were shapes of strange creatures flying around the cavern and brushing against her but she kept moving, looking at her feet as best she could. Finally, she stood stock still and looked up. Amongst all the evil shapes flying around the cavern, there was The Great Owl! It looked pleased for the first time and seemed to be beckoning. She followed.

Then the floor gave way beneath her feet, and she began to fall, but her back and sides and legs seemed to make contact with a solid wall, as if she were falling down a huge tube. She had taken her eyes off her feet, and this was how people who failed the tunnel died, by breaking the most important rule of all. She was certain this was the end. She felt tears pouring down her cheeks; after all that she had been through, this was it – finished! Faster and faster she went. After a while, despair overtook her, and it was almost a comfort to accept her death. A strange feeling of peace came upon her. Death would be the end of all her suffering.

***

Suddenly, the total darkness was replaced by a shattering bright light; she was hurtling through space. The light was too bright for Valda to open her eyes and though it was just a few seconds, it seemed much longer. Finally, she splashed into beautiful, warm water. She sank for half a minute or more, and then began to ascend. Her lungs were bursting as she rose ever higher and faster until she reached the surface, coughing and choking. The light was dazzling to her eyes which had been accommodated to the dark.

Then there was a strange noise which at first she could not understand. Slowly, through dim memories, she recognized it; it was the sound of people cheering! She slowly swam to the side of the small lake, and there she was greeted by a crowd of cheering and clapping people. A man came forward and put a purple cloak around her shoulders. She could see others, so many of them looking familiar, yet somehow different. They looked so young and beautiful, for they had not lived in the valley for many years. Even now, Valda felt the healing power of this place, wherever it was, as so many came forward with garlands of flowers to lay on her.

***

The sky was blue. To Valda, who had not seen the real, true sky for so long, it was paradise – blue heaven. Thoughts of the horrors of the tunnel and even the pains of her wounds slowly evaporated, leaving her to soak in the beauty of this new sky, distracted only by the exquisite greens of the plants rejoicing under the golden sun. To Valda, this was indeed paradise itself! Having survived The Tunnel, she knew that she could stay here for some happy years, but she also knew in her heart that no-one could stay in paradise forever. The Black Rat would have its way in the end, but the joy of this wondrous present could never be erased and her arrival would live on in the stars.

Journey into the P-Zone

Commander Alban Stone checked the time; as usual, he was ahead of schedule for his appointment. He felt perfectly calm and indeed was looking forward to the few minutes of 'inner solitude' before the interview. He had done the necessary pre-reading and if the job was offered to him – researching the further understanding of the P-Zone – then he would leap at the chance. 'Yes,' he mused to himself, 'the P-Zone is certainly a wonderful area of study.' There was no other unexplained phenomenon in the whole of cosmology more deserving of attention.

It had first been noticed some 50 years earlier when astronauts touching the Outer Limits would sometimes go insane for no apparent reason. The earlier explanations – still not entirely discredited – were that the P-Zone phenomenon was rather like the water mirage experience when people spent time in the desert. However, unlike the excruciating thirst and the mirroring effect of the sands which produced the visual hallucination of water, here it was thought to be the personal and spiritual solitude which produced the hallucinations.

Heaven and Hell, God and Satan, and a pageant of devils and angels – and worse – reduced the traveller to a trembling ghost of his former self; no-one who experienced the P-Zone psychosis ever returned to a normal life.

***

However, there were some strange inconsistencies in the phenomenon. Firstly, although mentally super-healthy travellers had some resistance, it was extremely difficult to predict who would suffer and who would be spared the experience. Secondly, different parts of the Explored Universe had different potential for producing it... the universe was still full of diversity, mystery and intrigue.

***

Alban Stone stared thoughtfully at the huge blue screen in front of him, enjoying his 'inner solitude' and awaiting with interest the interview.

The screen finally rose up, revealing the five Savants who gave him their full attention. Some water was sipped, and perhaps it was this noise which made Stone opens his eyes.

"Greetings, Commander Stone, and many congratulations on being selected for this interview." The atmosphere appeared cold, but this was business; the love for all society members was a given, like under-floor heating.

"First I must ask about your understanding of the P-Zone problem."

Maybe this was a loosener question like in the old days, or maybe it was to check that he had done his research.

Alban answered in some detail about the state of knowledge of the P-Zone, eyes unswervingly glued to the questioner except for just an occasional glance at the other panel members whose eyes remained fixed on him.

"Are you aware of any differences between Sector 18 and the P-Zone psychosis?" asked Savant number 2.

He replied that there were great sector variations in the penetrance of the psychosis, but he was unaware of the details of Sector 18.

Savant 2 smiled wryly. "The penetrance in Sector 18 is 100%."

Alban was surprised; travellers in dangerous zones could use axillary patches for emergencies. They stuck to the skin of the armpit and could be massaged to release sedative drugs into the bloodstream to help the traveller cope with some of the terrors.

Savant 2 read Alban's mind and added, with a look of some perplexion, "And the patches have no effect whatsoever in Sector 18 – none! What do you think of that?"

Alban thought for a moment and smiled: "That is wonderful. After all, the difficulties in researching the P-Zone are the unpredictabilities. Now, at last, we have real scientific opportunities to discover more about it; a place in the universe where the P-Zone psychosis is certain to happen."

The Screen came down, almost instantaneously.

Alban wondered if he had failed the interview, but after a few seconds knew that reflection was unhelpful and went back into his inner solitude.

**

"He is the one," said Savant 5. "He is the only one who can achieve this mission." They all nodded apart from Savant 4 who became aware of their gaze. "It will destroy him... I find it hard to condemn such a clean heart to such a fate," she said sadly.

"Yet the pods must be dispersed into Sector 18 for the continuance of the Earthrace," adjoined Savant 2. "The task must be done, though the chances of success are uncertain, and the destruction of Commander Stone a certainty!"

"Not quite a certainty," replied Savant 3, and then almost like a teacher continued:

"We know that the cosmic force which infiltrates Sector 18 penetrates into the ship and induces a profound inner turmoil in our traveller which compels him to abort the mission. By sending our traveller back to us in a state of insanity, this cosmic force could even be trying to tell us something? Could our most perfect human being withstand these attacks? We just do not know! All we can be certain of is that we have chosen the most perfect subject for the test; Commander Stone is the only one. He is The One who will be able to deliver the pods – of that I have no doubt. Whether he will come back unbroken is unlikely, but we must take the chance."

**

The curtain drew up, and Alban opened his eyes.

"Well?" asked the Savants.

"If I am selected, then with gratitude and excitement I volunteer for the mission."

The Savants stood and saluted him. Alban could not see the tears in the eyes of two of them. There had not been another candidate for the mission. He was their only hope: he was The One.

***

These missions had to be single-person. Alban thought about earlier missions which had had many crew members and how inefficient they had been. Biological support systems were very demanding of load and area, and hence single person missions had become standard. Moreover, the pre-programmed flight gave human interventions a tiny role. Naturally, there must be some human presence, or the craft could be taken over by unforeseen events and indeed the rare human interventions – when needed – could avert a catastrophe.

The computer update buzzed on, "84 yaeons into our flight."

The computer voice was the voice of his old Psychology Professor who Alban had dearly loved. Computer voice profiles were calculated so that the interest and feel-good factor of the traveller would be best served.

"All is going according to plan. We will approach the outer edge of the P-Zone in 7 yaeons, and the pods will be automatically discharged into Sector 18 at 107 yeaons; then we will return at increasing velocity. All biological parameters, Alban, are entirely normal. No unexpected forces within scanning range. Space is clear and travel conditions are perfect."

"Anything at all unusual to report?" asked Alban.

"Nothing whatsoever... except..." it seemed that the computer was reluctant to continue.

"Do carry on," said Alban smiling.

"Your behaviour is outside of normal with no request of comfort view or fantasy support."

"That is okay," said Alban, "mark that down as normal."

Commander Stone settled down into his inner solitude to await his challenge.

***

"Your behaviour is abnormal. Your behaviour is abnormal. Your behaviour is abnormal," intoned the computer with increasing agitation.

Alban looked at the figure floating in front of him. It was an image from deep in his subconscious – maybe from childhood – of some evil spirit. He smiled; this was entirely as expected – hallucinations produced by the aliens of Sector 18. The figure would have been terrifying in any context, but Alban reached back into his inner solitude.

"What do you want?" he asked the figure.

"We want you to stay away from our sector," snarled the spirit, the spittle dribbling off his yellow teeth which looked poised to strike.

"We have no fear of evil," smiled Alban, half his mind locked into the inner solitude. "We come in peace. If you are of Evil, we will fight you until we win; if you are Good then we will bring goodness to you, and together we will make the universe more hallowed."

The devil-spirit howled in pain and anguish, and Alban watched as it writhed and contorted, as though trying to escape from its own skin. Slowly it began to change – first the colours, then the shape; the transformation was far more terrifying than any horrors from any nightmare. Alban withdrew into his inner solitude. Shortly afterwards, his eyes opened and he beheld a sight that would forever be burned into his brain.

"The pods will be discharged shortly," said the computer voice, but Alban was lost... lost in a new, terrifying, and surreal world.

**

The five Savants were older but still quite recognisable. Like old soldiers discussing their war experiences, they could lapse into a true friendship now their sacred tasks were complete.

"Alban Stone," reflected Savant 3, "I do think that he was the most perfect human being we ever had the privilege to interview."

"Yes... and we ordered his destruction!" added Savant 4.

"Yes we did," said Savant 1, "but we really did have no choice."

They all nodded.

"The pods were delivered to Sector 18 and thus far there have been no further incursions... it was a success... in some ways the most successful mission of our jurisdiction."

How often had they repeated these words to each other – by way of reassurance for destroying a wonderful being? For did not Commander Stone say that he wanted to understand the P-Zone and still they were none the wiser? Of course, he himself was oblivious to all of this. When each of the Savants had visited him singly or as a group, not a word would escape his lips, just an expression of total bliss on his face... the face of a man who believed he had experienced the ultimate. He truly did belong in the monastery (there were still a few around) where he lived the simple, frugal life of the monk and appeared seemingly at peace with himself. Like all travellers to the P-Zone in Sector 18, the hallucinations had made him incapable of normal life afterward.

It remained unknown why the mission had been so successful. Perhaps the alien forces were powers for the greater good of the universe and had been persuaded by the purity of Alban's soul? Perhaps it is only at the very boundaries of our universe that humans could access profound spiritual experiences. But what if Sector 18 were the interface where Good and Evil meet and maybe (one hesitates to even say it) Alban Stone really did "gaze upon the face of God?"

The Last Job

Genius can take many forms and the contortions of his life that had led to his current position would captivate the attention of any criminologist for many a year.

Branner reflected on his "empire," and on his "Aladdin's Cave" – an invisible, secret fortress drilled from the granite beneath the city – hidden from the searching eyes of the authorities and especially the police. Not only was his citadel-fortress unknown to the government and undetectable by any of their instruments; the electronic devices which guarded any possible entry-point made this haven ultra-secure.

Theoretically, of course, there was always the risk of someone informing the authorities, but Branner knew his people; they had all passed the loyalty test, and even if their love and loyalty wavered, the inevitable nemesis that would come down upon them would be the ultimate loyalty guarantee. Yes, this was a safe haven! He looked around the room, bedecked with the "fruits of his labours" – the paintings, the sculptures, the original objets d'art worth millions – maybe billions – that he had "acquired" over the last three decades. Yet his greatest treasures were the electronic ones and his genius at making his home an electronic palace – the best sound systems, advanced diapsid screens, even the rainbow quoron lasers in the aquarium were of his own doing... yes this was truly a paradise.

And his companions? Brilliant people to the last man. Max over there had helped him to the further reaches of electronics, Tyndall with code-breaking and electronic communication (and disruption!), Danielle his personal trainer and climbing adviser... they had all played their part. Even his sons – Sven the tax lawyer and Bosworth the bankruptcy consultant – had turned out well.

A gentle croaking seemed to come from Branner's tiepin:

"Okay, Guardian, let in Devon and Alex."

"Check," replied the mechanical voice. The double security of voice-recognition electronics and personal identification pass-checks had been in force for years down here but were only just reaching consciousness in even the most techno-aware circles.

***

He looked around at his adoring audience, stroked his lapel, and a loud noise like the tapping of a spoon on a table sounded.

"I've brought you all here on this very special occasion for my farewell party. This is a party of thanks to all of you whose brilliance and loyalty has made my life so rich and fulfilling. And tonight I wish to announce my retirement from my life of..." he paused, "crime." The final word was said with a rising inflection, like a question.

They smiled but did not applaud. Branner had been a hero and an icon to so many people. He was truly beloved by his inner circle and had inspired so many to greater prosperity.

"But," he said, "I have promised myself one last hurrah." This vocation of mine has brought me such joy, excitement, and delights that I must retire on a really high note – a perfect way to end my career... and I need your help!

He looked around pensively, before catching each individual's eyes.

"What should it be? Yes, what would be a fitting climax to my career?"

He paused to let his colleagues savour the drama of the moment. "Brothers and sisters, there is only one possible venue for my last performance... to burgle the 'castle' of Howard Sturgess."

There was a stunned silence in which the very walls of the room seemed to share. Then there was a ripple of applause which led to a cheer and then a standing ovation. They all knew that this would be the ultimate challenge and that each one of their skills would be vital.

"It can be done. It will be done," he said, imitating perfectly the voice of Howard Sturgess. They all laughed appreciatively.

***

In fact, a raid on Howard Sturgess's home had been Branner's first big job, and it was largely because of the incredibly advanced technological inventions which he had stolen from Sturgess that he had become the master criminal of his era. Sturgess had since become very famous himself, a true celebrity and a legend, though he remained a shadowy figure with connections both in the international underworld and indeed in his own government.

"In the meantime, please, please raise your glasses in a toast to my last job!" continued Branner.

"The last job!" they all toasted with enthusiasm followed by heartfelt applause for this great and inspiring leader.

***

Three months! Yes, it had taken three whole months to prepare for the task fully! As always, nothing had been left to chance and only when the whole team was satisfied could the green light be given. Sturgess was out of the country in his role as the keynote speaker at the International Counter-Terrorism Conference in Beirut; Branner's web was everywhere, and his hack into the iris check at the airport was the definitive proof of Sturgess's departure.

He stood outside Sturgess's 'Castle.'

The total blackness was, of course, irrelevant with his enhanced infrared goggles as he climbed up the sheer face of the 'burglar-proof' wall. He was clad in a sensor-invisible dolce-suit stolen from the CIA; 'stealth technology gone personal' as he had explained to his team. Even so, he must not look up, or the protection would be gone; the climb had to be measured instrumentally. The sensors on his wrist pack would pick up any warning detectors, but he already had a total picture of what anti-burglary devices might be in place from Tyndall's surveillance and electronic infiltration reports. Cautious? Yes, but heck, this was the last job and there was no room for the slightest hitch. The usual predicted booby traps he despatched with ease and with no increase in his heart rate, and even the guard dogs – ferocious as they appeared – he knew were merely brilliant holograms; Sturgess was legendary for his holographic innovations and his passion for dogs was known to all.

Suddenly there was a deafening alarm – a screeching siren – going off all around. Branner froze, took a deep breath and tried to think rationally. Sturgess was out of the country – yes! Sturgess would not want the police alerted with the possibility of them prying into his private fortress – correct! So what could this be? "Remember," Travis had advised, "do not trust your senses!"

Branner remained totally calm and collected his thoughts; finally, he moved just 20 centimetres to the right, and the sound disappeared. This was focussed multi-stereo ultrasound – small sounds from multiple sources focussed on the area of his path. He looked down and smiled: "Best stay off the obvious track," he thought to himself, quietly applauding the elegance of the "Whispering Gallery Effect" so beautifully used by Sturgess.

Then, suddenly, the wall collapsed under his feet and his world began to spin wildly into a vortex of terror and uncertainty.

"Do not trust your senses," he repeated to himself, "a wall made by Sturgess could never collapse." He tried to ignore the messages from his brain and continued the climb using nothing but his directions from the sensors. Finally, the sensations disappeared. He shook his head in disbelief and admiration; Sturgess had somehow used oscillating magnetic fields to target the semi-circular canals of his own innate gyroscope system in the brain. Totally brilliant – low cost, permanently there and for any ordinary burglar – an instantly terminated climb.

***

He climbed over the balcony, frished open the lock, switched on the light, and surveyed the room.

The worst was surely over! Then he noticed a hunched figure sitting by the fireplace.

"Good evening, Mr Branner," said Sturgess quietly.

***

Branner froze. How could this be? Sturgess was definitely – absolutely definitely – in Beirut. "Do not trust your senses," he repeated to himself.

"You are the only one who could beat my defences," said Sturgess. "I always knew that you would return some day."

Branner stared at the figure; could this be a look-alike? No, Sturgess would never allow another soul into his inner chamber. It must be Sturgess – but how?

"What do you want me to do now?" he asked the figure.

"Well, this is a party, and you must leave early with your prize; it is by the curtains on the way out. I wish you no harm. Good night, Mr Branner."

Branner turned, walked towards the curtains and the exit totally despondent; he had been defeated.

But something niggled; his data and preparations had all been perfect... what had gone wrong? He had studied Sturgess – everything – his mannerisms, appearance, idiosyncrasies, areas of interest.

Branner sat down on the balcony to collect his thoughts. "This just has to be a hologram – but the most perfect hologram on the planet – an electronic replication of everything about Sturgess."

Even so, what could he do to switch it off? In his mind, he went through everything he knew of Sturgess's vocal expressions. 'What would the verbal command be to switch off the hologram guard?'

He thought for 20 minutes, though it seemed like several hours, then walked back into the room and said in a very accurate impersonation of Sturgess's voice, "Call off the dogs!" The apparition disappeared leaving an eerie silence and whatever treasures were there at Branner's mercy.

***

The 'hit-room' was beautiful even in the infrared view and there was no need to rush: here was a man in total control of the situation.

Since the first burglary, Sturgess had certainly done very well for himself with fine-looking furnishings costing millions, but the safe itself was a big disappointment just diamonds and a few documents. Branner would take the diamonds, of course, but would certainly not rob his 'benefactor' of the documents, which were of no use to him anyway.

He sat with his chin in his hands in total disappointment. Had Sturgess stopped inventing? Did he store his real valuables in a bank vault? What would he, Branner, do if he were in Sturgess's position? This whole thing just did not make sense. If you were the world's greatest (well, damn near!) inventor, why would you entrust your treasures to a bank? The treasures simply must be here somewhere in this room. But where?

He tried to remember if anything was different about the room, but although he had a feeling that something was changed, he could not truly remember. The treasures must be in this room, but they are not in this room!

He looked around again. Ah – maybe he had built a false wall in front of the old one? Yes, that would certainly explain it! Yes – and we can check that with the depth scanner! Branner checked every area of the room – even the outer facing walls for depth with the scanner. Nothing! Nothing! The scanner showed they were solid.

Branner sat down again. He still had hours of time left. There had to be some explanation. He checked in his pocket database for the expected dimensions of the room, and then scanned them – a perfect match! There were *definitely* no false walls.

The floor – what if there was a false floor? Branner checked the height of the room from his database and did a scan – a complete match! Yet... something in his distant memory told him that there was something different about the dimensions of the room.

Suddenly a thrill of understanding shot through his spine; what if this was a phase-change simulated floor? This would fool his sensors! His admiration for Sturgess almost brought tears to his eyes... if only things had been different and they could have worked together... but what should he do now?

Burgess sat and thought. In his early days, he would check for false fronts and hollowness by tapping – the way doctors examine a patient's chest – a technique called "percussion." The middle finger is laid firmly against the surface to be tested and this finger is tapped with the middle finger of the other hand; the sound and the feel tells the doctor whether the lungs are diseased – or in the case of the burglar whether there is a false wall.

Excited, Branner began his "percussion" of the floor. At the first strike, it was clear there was something unusual – a strange tingle and a thump were clearly discerned. Yes, that was it! A false electronic floor!

"Howard, I love you," murmured the ecstatic Branner. But what to do about it? The aerial circuit disrupter would certainly 'remove' the floor (and the drop to the real floor would be small) but would this trigger some other response?

Branner reflected on the character of Sturgess and guessed that, in his arrogance, he would probably believe that his electronic floor would be totally undetectable. But dare he risk the final challenge? The thought of going home 'empty-handed' finally persuaded him; his hands trembled as he fired the circuit disrupter...

***

"My God!" cried Branner as the floor capsized beneath him. The drop was small as anticipated, but there in the corner were the treasures! There could be no doubt! He gathered them up speedily, put them into his sack and began to clamber quickly down the slippery wall, not forgetting the 'present' that the holographic Sturgess had offered. All was quiet except for the barking of the holographic dogs and the noise of the city beneath him.

***

As he had promised, the 'second retirement party' was soon scheduled – and eagerly awaited by all. Branner narrated the entire experience to an enthralled and adoring audience, with absolute detail and some humour. No-one else would have even attempted, and certainly no-one could have achieved, this final feat of Branner.

A feeling of achievement – almost of invincibility – pervaded the atmosphere. Branner was happy; a true feeling of fulfilment, yet somehow tinged with a slight sadness, that this was it. The game was all done and finished, and though he left as the victor, he would never again have to face the mighty challenges which had punctuated his career.

The 'booty' was on display for all to see; though only Max and Tyndall were really able to appreciate how advanced and usable they might be.

"And we are pretty sure," said Branner, "...that is, Max, Tyndall, and I are pretty sure, that this trove will ensure the success of our enterprise for many years to come." Everyone applauded generously.

"As yet, of course, we don't know the use of some of them, but this thing," he said, holding aloft a beautiful symmetrical crystal "is totally astonishing." He waved around an object the size of a large grapefruit that looked like a perfect diamond. "It may well be a diamond," he went on, "though Jennifer says she isn't sure!" Jennifer was the diamond expert in the group; if she wasn't sure, this was certainly something incredibly unusual. Everyone stared at the beautiful "diamond" in awe; it almost seemed to glow a blue-white colour from its depths.

"Also," Branner went on, his enthusiasm getting the better of him, "this device here is of massive interest." He picked up what looked like a huge piece of plasticine. "At first, we thought it might be explosive, but it certainly isn't. We think the soft covering is to absorb all frequencies of the spectrum other than the selected one, and the controls inside can be selective in reception and transmission." He paused for a moment, poking around in the plasticine. "Ah here it is," he finally said, and a click announced that he had activated one of the controls. He remained transfixed looking into it.

"And this thing," continued Branner, holding a large oblong box, "we believe is some kind of generator, but it must be something quite unusual as Sturgess is certainly a genius – possibly the second greatest innovator on earth," he smiled wryly. "Second only to us," he added to laughter and applause.

Everyone felt the power of the triumphant victory – like Gods upon the Earth. The laughter and the feel-good of it all, fuelled by the drinks, made everyone feel beautifully relaxed. In their blissful states, no-one noticed as the crystal began to glow even more brightly and a barely visible gas began to escape from the oblong container. They all felt so wonderfully serene; such moments of triumph were the very best of times after all.

After a few minutes, the lights flickered momentarily, and there was a croaking sound. Branner thought he heard his own voice say "Thank you Guardian, you can let in our special guests," but the mood of the party overtook him once more.

The strange mist was slowly pervading the room. Danielle was the first to fall asleep, then Max and Tyndall looked at each other in horror as the truth began to dawn on them. But, it was too late, like the rest they fell into a deep and untroubled 'hibernation'.

***

When they awoke, the mist had gone and so had everything else – everything! All the trophies from Sturgess's castle, every single thing from all those years of work – all gone. All that was left was a note pinned to Branner's jacket. It read: "Congratulations, Mr Branner; you almost made it." It was signed Howard Sturgess.

Branner stared in disbelief at the scene. His friends slowly began to awaken trying to make sense of the picture of total ruin.

Branner was devastated; this was the work of Sturgess at his best and he – Branner – had been outsmarted, and out-technologied; this was the worst defeat of his entire life.

For several minutes, Branner held his head in his hands in total despair, and then something began to stir inside him – a deep inner voice of hope, for Branner lived on hope and optimism. Yes, he had lost this battle and Sturgess had the spoils. But now he could go back to the drawing board and start all over from the beginning; 'the game is on again' he smiled to himself.

Lightning Source UK Ltd.
Milton Keynes UK
UKOW06f1506141217
314459UK00006B/158/P